P9-DHJ-312

The Christmas Ranch

RaeAnne Thayne

HARLEQUIN® SPECIAL EDITION®

If you purchased this book without a cover you should be aware
that this book is stolen property. It was reported as "unsold and
destroyed" to the publisher, and neither the author nor the
publisher has received any payment for this "stripped book."

Recycling programs
for this product may
not exist in your area.

ISBN-13: 978-0-373-65853-4

The Christmas Ranch

Copyright © 2014 by RaeAnne Thayne

All rights reserved. Except for use in any review, the reproduction
or utilization of this work in whole or in part in any form by any
electronic, mechanical or other means, now known or hereinafter
invented, including xerography, photocopying and recording, or in
any information storage or retrieval system, is forbidden without
the written permission of the publisher, Harlequin Enterprises Limited,
225 Duncan Mill Road, Don Mills, Ontario M3B 3K9, Canada.

This is a work of fiction. Names, characters, places and incidents are
either the product of the author's imagination or are used fictitiously, and
any resemblance to actual persons, living or dead, business establishments,
events or locales is entirely coincidental.

This edition published by arrangement with Harlequin Books S.A.

For questions and comments about the quality of this book, please contact us
at CustomerService@Harlequin.com.

® and TM are trademarks of Harlequin Enterprises Limited or its corporate
affiliates. Trademarks indicated with ® are registered in the United States Patent
and Trademark Office, the Canadian Intellectual Property Office and in other
countries.

Printed in U.S.A.

www.Harlequin.com

RAEANNE THAYNE,

New York Times and USA TODAY bestselling author, finds inspiration in the beautiful northern Utah mountains, where she lives with her husband and three children. Her books have won numerous honors, including RITA® Award nominations from Romance Writers of America and a Career Achievement Award from RT Book Reviews. RaeAnne loves to hear from readers and can be contacted through her website, www.raeannethayne.com.

To my wonderful readers,
for sharing this amazing journey with me.
I consider myself extraordinarily blessed that
I can spend my days spinning stories with
happy endings, while hoping that my words might
make someone's day a little brighter. Thank you!

Chapter One

Though Thanksgiving was still a week and a half away, Christmas apparently had already rolled into Pine Gulch, Idaho, in all its snowy glory.

Hope Nichols looked through the windshield of the crappy old Ford pickup truck she had picked up for a cool thousand dollars at the edge of a Walmart parking lot in Salt Lake City. On a late afternoon in November the storefronts of the small but vibrant downtown area were alive with Christmas displays—trees, lights, toy soldiers, the occasional Nativity scene.

As she drove through more residential areas on her way to Cold Creek Canyon, she saw the holiday spirit extended here. Nearly every house had decorations of some sort, from inflatable snowmen to a full-fledged Santa and reindeer display.

She didn't mind even the kitschiest of decorations, even though to some it might seem early in the season. Considering she hadn't spent the holidays at home for the past five years—or even in the country—she couldn't wait to embrace the whole Christmas thing this year.

She supposed that was a good thing, since her family's Ranch was the holiday epicenter around here.

This area of eastern Idaho already had a few inches of snow—not much, but enough to cover everything in a lovely blanket of white and add a bit of seasonal charm to the town she remembered with such warmth and affection.

While Pine Gulch wasn't exactly her hometown, it was close enough. Hope and her sisters had lived here through most of their formative teen years, and she loved every inch of it, from the distant view of the west slope of the Tetons to the unassuming storefronts to the kind people who waved at her even now, though they couldn't possibly recognize her *or* the old blue pickup truck with the primer on the side.

She had come to be pretty fond of the old Ford. It didn't exactly drive like a dream, but it had four-wheel drive and all its working parts. Buying it had been an impulsive decision—she had intended to rent a car in Salt Lake City to drive home after she flew in from northern Africa, but had suddenly realized she would need transportation permanently now. This truck would get her through the gnarly winter season until she figured out what she would do next. After a decade of wandering, she was ready to stay put for a while.

Nerves in her stomach danced a little, as they had been doing throughout the five-hour drive from Salt Lake, while she tried to anticipate the reaction she would find at the Star N Ranch when she showed up out of the blue with her duffel bag.

Aunt Mary would probably cry, her older sister, Faith, would be shocked and her younger sister, Celeste, would smile in that quiet way of hers.

The children would at least be happy to see her, though she knew Louisa and Barrett—and everyone else, for that matter—were still reeling from the death of their father. Travis, Faith's husband and childhood sweetheart, had died four months earlier in a tragic accident. Hope had come back for his funeral, of course, but her correspondence and video chats with her family since then had mostly been superficial.

It was time to come home. Past time. Since Travis's death, she couldn't shake the feeling that her family needed her, despite their protests that all was fine. The holiday season was insane at The Christmas Ranch and all hands were necessary, even when those hands belonged to the wanderer in the fam—

Whack!

With a noise as loud as a gunshot, something hit the passenger-side window of her truck, jerking her thoughts back to the present. In the space of a heartbeat, the window shattered as Hope slammed on the brakes, ducked and instinctively yelled a curse word her mostly Berber students taught her.

What the...?

Who would be shooting at her? For a crazy moment, she was a terrified, desperate thirteen-year-old girl again, heart pounding, adrenaline pulsing. She didn't have flashbacks very often, but when she did, they could roll over her like a bulldozer.

She drew in a breath, forcing away the panic. This was Pine Gulch. There were no snipers here, no rebel factions. Nobody would be shooting at her. She glanced at the window. Because the truck was older, it didn't have tempered glass and the entire window had shattered. All she found was a melting pile of snow amid the shattered glass—and a healthy-sized rock.

Not a gunshot, then. A dirty trick. Tentatively, she raised her head to look around. At first, she didn't see anything, until a flurry of movement on that side of the vehicle caught her gaze.

A young boy stood just off the road looking shocked and not a little guilty.

Hope pulled over to the side of the road then jumped out of the driver's side and headed for him.

The kid stared at her, eyes wide. He froze for only a moment as she approached, then whirled around and took off at top speed across the snow-covered lawn just as a man walked around the side of the house with a couple of snow shovels in hand.

"You're in luck, kid," he called. "I found shovels for each of us."

The man's voice trailed off as the boy raced behind him, using what were quite impressive muscles as a shield, as if he thought Hope was going to start hurling snowball-covered rocks right back at him.

"Hey. Come back here. Where do you think you're going, young man?" she demanded sternly in her best don't-mess-with-me teacher's voice.

The big man frowned and set the snow shovels blade-down on the sidewalk. "Excuse me, lady. What the he—er, heck is your problem?"

She told herself her heart was racing only from adrenaline at her window suddenly shattering. It had nothing to do with this large, muscled, *gorgeous* man with short dark hair and remarkable hazel eyes. Somehow he seemed even bigger as he bristled at her, overpowering and male.

She, however, had gone against bullies far worse than some small-town cowboy with a juvenile delinquent and an attitude.

She pointed to the pickup truck, engine still running, and the shattered passenger window.

"Your son here is the problem—or more accurately, the rock he just tossed through my window. I could have been seriously hurt. It's a miracle I didn't run off the road."

"I'm not his son," the kid snapped. He looked angry and belligerent at the very idea.

She supposed it was only natural her mind immediately went to kidnapping, especially after the sudden flashback.

"You're not?"

"I'm his uncle," Sexy Dude said, with a frustrated look at the boy. "Did you see him throw it? I'm sure you must be mistaken. Joey is not the kind of kid who would throw a rock at a moving vehicle—especially a *stranger's* moving vehicle."

Was he trying to convince her or himself? His words rang a little hollow, making her wonder if Joey was *exactly* the kind of kid who would vandalize a vehicle, whether he knew the owners or not.

"Then explain to me why my window is shattered and why he took off the moment I stopped my truck to talk to him about it."

The guy frowned. "Joe. Tell the nice lady you didn't throw a rock at her window."

The boy lifted his chin obstinately but after meeting her gaze for just a moment, he looked down at his snowboots. "I didn't throw a rock," he insisted, then added in a muffled sort of aside, "It was a snowball."

"A snowball with a rock inside it," she retorted.

He looked up and gave his uncle an imploring look. "It was a accident. I didn't mean to, Uncle Rafe. I swear."

"Joey." The uncle said the single name with a defeated kind of frustration, making her wonder what the situation was between the two of them. Where were the boy's parents?

"It was a accident," he repeated. Whether it was genuine or an act, Joey now sounded like he was going to cry.

"*An* accident," she corrected.

"Whatever," the boy said.

"Using proper English is important when you wish to convey your point." Yes, she sounded prim but six years of combined experience in the Peace Corps and teaching English across the globe had ingrained habits that were probably going to be tough to break.

"Okay. It was *an* accident," he spoke with such dramatic exaggeration that she almost smiled, until she remembered the crisis at hand.

"That's better, but I'm still not sure I believe you. I think you were aiming right at my truck."

"I didn't mean to break the window. I wasn't even

trying to hit the window, I was trying to hit the hub-cap. My friend Samantha and me are playing a game and we get five points for every hubcap."

"My friend Samantha and I," she said. She couldn't seem to help herself, even though she noticed the correction only made the uncle glower harder, making him look big and rough-edged and even more dangerous.

She suddenly felt small and not nearly as tough as she liked to think.

"Can we deep six the English lessons, lady, and focus on your window?"

She was nervous, she suddenly realized. Was it because of his military haircut or the muscles or because he was so great-looking? She pushed away the uneasiness and forced herself to concentrate on the real issue.

"Sorry. Reflex. I'll stop now. I've been teaching English in northern Africa the past few years and was in the Peace Corps before that. I'm just returning to Pine Gulch to visit my family. They live in Cold Creek Canyon and…"

Her voice trailed off. He didn't care about that. She cleared her throat. "Right. My window. It was a very dangerous thing you did, young man. Tell your friend Samantha it's a bad idea to throw snowballs at cars, whether the snowballs have rocks in them or not. You could distract the driver and someone could easily get hurt—maybe even you."

The boy gave her a pugnacious sort of look but said nothing until his uncle nudged him.

"Tell the nice lady you're sorry."

"I don't think she's very nice," he grumbled.

Again, Hope almost smiled, until she met the man's gaze and found him looking extremely unamused by the entire situation.

Humorless jerk.

"Too bad." The boy's uncle—Rafe, was it?—frowned at him. "Tell her you're sorry anyway."

Joey looked down at the snow-covered ground again and then finally met her gaze. "I'm sorry I hit your window and not your hubcap. We don't get any points for hitting windows."

As apologies went, it was a little weak but she would still take it. She was suddenly weary of the whole situation and wanted to continue on toward the Star N and her family.

"In your defense, that window had a crack in it anyway. It probably wouldn't have shattered if it hadn't been for that."

"You're not going to be throwing any snowballs at cars again," the boy's uncle said sternly. "And you're going to tell Samantha not to do it either, right?"

"But I was winning the contest! She was gonna give me her new Darth Vader LEGO minifig if I won and I was gonna give her my Green Ninja minifig if *she* won."

"Too bad. The lady is right. It's dangerous. Look at the trouble you've already caused!"

The boy didn't look happy about it but he finally shrugged. "Fine."

"We'll pay for the window replacement, of course. If you get an estimate, you can have them send the bill to me here. Rafe Santiago. I'll warn you that I'm only going to be in town for another few weeks, though."

The name seemed to strike a chord deep in her subconscious. Had they met before? Something about his hazel eyes—striking against his burnished skin—reminded her of someone but she couldn't seem to pin down who or where.

She didn't remember any Santiagos living in this little house before. From what she remembered of Hope's Crossing, this had always been a rental house, often used short-term for seasonal workers and such.

"I will do that." She held out her hand, deciding there was no reason they couldn't leave on good terms. "I'm Hope Nichols. You can find me at The Christmas Ranch, in Cold Creek Canyon."

At her words, something sparked in those hazel eyes but she couldn't identify it.

"Nichols?" he said sharply.

"Yes."

Perhaps he knew her sisters, though Faith went by her married name now, Dustin, and she couldn't imagine quiet, introverted Celeste having much to do with a rough and tumble man like him. Maybe Joey had caused trouble at the library where Celeste worked. She could believe that—though, okay, that might be a snap judgment.

"Can I go inside?" Joey asked. "Snow got in my boots and now my feet are *freezing*. I need to dump it out."

"Yeah. Go ahead. Dump the snow off on the porch, not inside."

Joey raced off and after a moment, Rafe Santiago—*why* was that name so familiar?—turned back to her.

"I'm sorry about my nephew," he said, rather

stiffly. "He's had a...rough time of it the past few weeks."

She wondered what had happened, but when he didn't volunteer any further details, she accepted it was none of her business. "I'm sorry if I came down too hard."

"I didn't say you did. Whatever he's been through isn't an excuse anyway. I'll talk to him about this stupid contest and make sure he and his friend both realize it's not a good idea."

He gave her another searching look and she had the strangest feeling he wanted to say something else. When the silence stretched between them, a little too long to be comfortable, she decided she couldn't wait around for him to speak.

"I should go. My family is waiting for me. I'll be in touch, Mr. Santiago."

"Rafe," he said gruffly. Was that his normal speaking voice or did she just bring out the rough edges? she wondered.

"Rafe. Nice to meet you, even under the circumstances."

She hurried back to her pickup truck and continued on toward home, though she couldn't shake the odd feeling that something momentous had just happened.

Rafe watched the taillights recede into the early evening gloom until she turned a corner and disappeared. Even then, he couldn't seem to make himself move, still reeling from the random encounter.

Hope Nichols.

Son of a bi...gun.

He checked the epithet. He was trying not to swear, even in his head. Joey didn't need any more bad habits. If Rafe didn't *think* the words, he wouldn't *speak* them. It was a logical theory but after twenty years in the navy, seventeen of those as a SEAL, cleaning up his language for the sake of a seven-year-old boy with an enormous chip on his shoulder was harder than he ever would have imagined.

He didn't have a choice. Like it or not—and he sure as he—er, heck, *didn't*—Joey was his responsibility now.

Hope Nichols. What were the odds?

He knew she and her sisters had come to live in Pine Gulch, Idaho, *after*. He might have been a green-as-alfalfa rookie who had never been on an actual mission before that tense December day seventeen years ago, but keeping track of the Nichols girls had been a point of honor.

They had an aunt and uncle here who had taken them in. He remembered being grateful for that, at least that they had *someone*. He had received a letter from the oldest, he remembered, a few months afterward...

The girl couldn't have been more than fourteen or fifteen but she had written to him like a polite old lady.

He had memorized the damn—er, darn—thing.

Dear Special Warfare Operator Santiago,
Thank you for participating in rescuing us from
Juan Pablo and his rebel group. You and the
other men in your navy SEAL platoon risked
your lives to save us. If not for you, we might

*still be in that awful camp. You are true Ameri-
can heroes. My sisters and I will never forget
what you have done for us.
Sincerely, Faith Marie Nichols.
PS: It is nobody's fault that our father died. We
don't blame anyone and know you tried your
best to save us all.*

The carefully written letter had been sweetly horrible and he had carried it around in his wallet for
years to remind him that navy SEALs couldn't afford even the smallest error in judgment.

Hope—the annoying grammarian with the ancient
pickup truck—had been the middle daughter, he remembered, all tangled blond hair and big, frightened
blue eyes. She had screamed when her father had
been shot, and the echo of that terrified, despairing
scream had haunted him for a long, long time.

He let out a breath. And now she was here, just a
few miles away from him, and he would have to in-
teract with her at least one more time.

Had she recognized him today? He couldn't be
sure. She had given him a strange look a few times,
as if she thought she knew him, but she hadn't said
anything.

Why hadn't he identified himself and explained
their old history?

He wasn't sure—maybe because the opportunity
hadn't really come up. How does a guy say, *Hey, I
know this is a strange coincidence but I was there the
day your family was rescued from terrorists nearly
two decades ago. Oh, and by the way, my inexperi-*

ence contributed to your father's death. Sorry about
that and your broken window, too.

He let out a breath, marveling again at the strange,
twisting corkscrews of fate that had brought him to
Pine Gulch, in such proximity to the Nichols sisters.
When Cami called him in tears and explained that
she had been arrested and that Joey had gone into
emergency foster care, he had known immediately
he had to help his nephew, whatever it took.

The fact that his path would bring him to Pine
Gulch, where the Nichols sisters had landed after the
tragedy of that Christmas day so long ago, hadn't really hit home until he drove into the city limits two
weeks ago.

In the midst of trying to settle into a routine with
his nephew, he had wondered during those two weeks
whether they were still in town and if he should try
to contact any of them—and now that decision had
been taken out of his hands by Hope.

That seemed to be a common theme to his life
the past month—being in a position that left him
few choices.

His life had changed dramatically in the past
month. He had left the only career he had ever known
in order to take on the responsibility for a troubled
seven-year-old who wanted nothing to do with him.

He was determined to do his best for Joey. The
poor kid hadn't been given very many breaks in life.

Rafe still couldn't quite believe how far his sister
had fallen, from an honor student in high school to
being tangled up with a man who had seduced her
into coming to Idaho and had then dragged her into
a life of drugs and crime.

He had done his best for his sister, had joined the navy the day he turned eighteen so he could support her and had sent money for her care to their aunt, who had taken her in—but apparently that effort hadn't been enough to provide the future he always wanted for her.

He had failed with Cami. Now he had to see if he could do a better job with her son.

He opened the door to the short-term rental he had found in Pine Gulch after Cami begged him to let Joey stay here until she was sentenced, which at this point was only a few weeks away.

Joey was sitting on the bench in the foyer with his boots and coat still on, as if he were bracing himself for the punishment he fully expected.

Rafe's heart, grizzled and tough from years of combat, couldn't help but soften just a little at his forlorn posture and expression.

"I didn't mean to break the mean lady's window," his nephew said again, his voice small.

The kid needed consequences in order to learn how his choices could have impact in others' lives. Rafe knew that, but sometimes this parenting thing sucked big-time when what he really wanted was to gather him close and tell him everything would be okay.

"You might not have meant to cause harm, but you saw what happened. You messed up, kid."

The irony of those words seemed to reach out and grab him by the throat. Joey's actions might have cost Hope Nichols a car window, something that easily could be replaced.

His actions toward her and her sisters had far more long-reaching consequences.

If his reflexes had been half a second faster, he could have taken out that jacked-up, trigger-happy rebel before the bastard squeezed off the shot that took her father forever.

"Will I have to pay for the window?" Joey asked. "I have eight dollars in my piggy bank. Will it be more than that?"

"We'll figure it out. Maybe I'll pay her and then you can work to pay me back."

The boy looked out the window. "I can shovel the snow."

"Hate to break it to you, but I was going to make you do that anyway. That's going to be one of your regular chores, helping me with that. We'll have to figure out how to pay back Ms. Nichols some other way."

As for the debt *he* owed her, Rafe knew there was no way he could repay her or her sisters.

Chapter Two

Something was very, very wrong.

Hope wanted to think she was only upset from the encounter with Rafe Santiago and his very cute but troublesome nephew. Perhaps she was overwrought as a natural by-product from first having her window shattered in such a shocking manner and then coming face-to-face with a big, dangerous-looking man.

But as she approached the Star N and especially The Christmas Ranch—her family's holiday-themed attraction that covered fifteen acres of the cattle ranch—she couldn't seem to shake the edgy, unsettled feeling.

Where was everyone? As she approached, she could see the parking lot in front of the charming and rustic St. Nicholas Lodge and it was completely empty, which made absolutely no sense.

There should at least be a maintenance crew getting ready for the season. It usually took several weeks before opening day—which traditionally happened with a grand lighting ceremony at dusk on the Friday after Thanksgiving—to spruce things up, touch up the paint, repair any damage done throughout the summer.

Instead, the place looked like a ghost town. All it needed were a few tumbleweeds blowing through to complete the picture.

Maybe everybody had simply gone home for the day, but she suddenly realized the reindeer enclosure was missing slats *and* reindeer, nor did it look like any of the colored lights had been hung on the fence or in the shrubs lining the road.

She drove farther down the road with cold air whistling in from the shattered window. As she approached the parking lot entrance, her stomach suddenly dropped and she hit the brakes.

A banner obscured the sign that usually read Welcome to The Christmas Ranch, where your holiday dreams come true.

In huge red letters on a white background, it read simply, Closed Indefinitely.

Closed. Indefinitely.

Shock rocketed through her faster than a speeding sleigh. Impossible! She couldn't believe it. Surely her sisters wouldn't have closed down The Christmas Ranch without telling her! This was a tradition, a gift from the Nichols family to the rest of Pine Gulch and this entire area of southeastern Idaho.

Families came from miles around to partake of the holiday spirit. All of it. The horse-drawn sleigh rides. The sledding hill. Visits with Santa Claus. The reindeer herd in the petting zoo and the gift shop filled with local handicrafts and the huge collection of Nativities, many which had been sent from around the world by her parents as they traveled around as missionaries.

Even the cheesy little animatronic Christmas village was a family favorite.

It was a place of magic and wonder, a little piece of holiday spirit for the entire community to enjoy.

How could her sisters and Auntie Mary close it, indefinitely or otherwise?

And how many shocks in the space of an hour could one woman endure? Her hands shook on the steering wheel as she drove the remaining three hundred feet to the driveway leading to the ranch house.

She drove up the winding road with her heart pounding. At the house—a rambling white two-story farmhouse with a wide front porch—she parked and stomped up the steps.

Though she was tempted to dramatically storm inside—she had spent all her teen years in this house, after all, and still considered it her own—she forced herself to stop at the front door and knock.

Though Aunt Mary still lived here with Faith, it was really her sister's house now and Hope didn't feel she had the right to just barge in. Living in other cultures most of her life, barring the years she spent here, had given her a healthy respect for others' personal space.

Nobody answered for a few moments. She was about to pound harder when the door suddenly opened. Instead of Faith or Auntie Mary, her nephew, Barrett, stood on the other side of the door.

At the sight of her, his darling face lit up with a joy that seemed to soothe all the ragged, battered edges of her spirit and made the whole long journey worthwhile.

"Aunt Hope! What are you doing here? I didn't even know you were coming!"

"I'm sure it will be a big surprise to everybody," she answered, a little grimly.

"The best, best, *best* kind," her sweetly loyal nephew claimed as he wrapped his arms around her waist. She hugged him, feeling better already—even as she thought of the last little boy she had encountered, who hadn't been nearly so enthusiastic about her presence.

"Oh, I missed you," he exclaimed.

"I missed you, too, potato bug."

Barrett was seven and most of their relationship had developed via email and the occasional video chat when the vast time zone conflicts could be worked out.

She hadn't received nearly enough of these hugs in her lifetime, she suddenly decided, with an almost painful aching for family and home.

"Who's at the door, Barrett?" she heard her sister call from the kitchen.

"Don't tell her," Hope said, managing a grin even though some part of her was still annoyed with her sister.

"Um, nobody," he answered back, obviously not good at coming up with fibs on the fly.

"How can it be nobody?" her older sister said, and Hope could almost hear the frown in her voice.

Holding a finger to her mouth for Barrett, she headed down the hall toward the kitchen where her sister's voice originated.

In the doorway, she caught a glimpse of Faith at the work island in the center of what was really command central of the house. Her sister's dark hair was held back in a messy ponytail and she looked tired, with deep circles under her eyes and lines of strain bracketing her mouth.

More of Hope's half-formed displeasure at her sister slipped away. Her sister had lost so much—everything!—and Hope hadn't been here for her.

"Seriously, Barrett. Who was at the door? Was it UPS again, delivering something for Auntie Mary?"

The boy giggled, a sweet, pure sound that drew Faith's attention from the vegetables she was cutting at the island. She looked up and her jaw sagged.

"Hope! What in the world?"

Hope mustered a smile. "Surprise."

Her sister wiped her hands on a dish towel and came toward her. Faith had lost weight. Hope was struck again by how fragile and slight she seemed, as if a sharp gust of wind from a December storm would blow her clear out to the barn.

Those lines around her mouth had been etched by pain, she suddenly realized. Her sister had lost the love her life, her childhood sweetheart, a mere four months earlier in a tragic accident and had barely had time to grieve. She would be reeling from the loss of her husband for a long time.

Travis Dustin had been killed after he had rolled

an all-terrain vehicle while rounding up cattle in the mountains. He hadn't been wearing a helmet and had been killed instantly, leaving behind Faith and their two children.

Hope still couldn't believe he was gone. If she closed her eyes, she could almost picture him the last time she saw him alive, nearly two years earlier when she had been able to come home briefly between assignments in time for New Year's Eve. He had been a dear friend as well as a beloved brother-in-law and his loss had hit her hard.

She had been here four months earlier for his funeral but had only been able to stay a few days. It hadn't been long enough.

Hope crossed to her sister and hugged her hard, wishing she could absorb some of her pain.

They were extremely close to each other and to Celeste, their sibling relationship forged through their unorthodox upbringing and the tragedy that had changed all of them so long ago.

Faith rested her cheek against Hope's. "Oh, what a wonderful surprise. I thought you were going on to Nepal after you finished your teaching stint in Morocco."

"That was the plan, but I decided to take a break for a few months to figure things out. I thought maybe, I don't know, I could take a rest from traveling. Maybe stay and help you out around here for a while."

"Oh. It will be so wonderful to have you here longer than a few days!"

"I thought I could stay through the holidays, if you'll have me."

While Faith smiled at her with apparent delight, Hope didn't miss the sudden wariness in her gaze. "This is your home, too. You're always welcome here, you know that."

She paused and gave Hope a searching look. "I guess you must have seen the sign at the Ranch on the way in."

Hope tried to summon a little of the anger that had accompanied her on the short drive to the ranch-house but it was impossible to dredge up more than a little kernel at this sister she had always loved and admired for her courage, her sweetness, her practicality—all the things Hope didn't have.

Her sister had suffered great pain and somehow continued to trudge on, though Hope had no idea how she was managing it.

"I saw the sign. I don't understand what it means."

"It means we're not opening The Christmas Ranch this year," Barrett announced, sounding just as disgruntled as Hope had been when she first spotted the empty parking lot.

She placed a hand on his shoulder. "That's what I suspected when I saw the sign. I still can't quite believe it. Why didn't you tell me?"

Faith's mouth compressed into a tight line. "I would have told you eventually, if you had asked how things were going with The Christmas Ranch, but I didn't see any point in stirring the pot when you weren't here anyway."

She couldn't blame her sister for that, she supposed. Her family had no reason to believe this year would be any different from the last handful, when she hadn't been able to manage coming home for longer than a day or two for a quick visit, if that.

"What gives, though? Why are we Closed Indefinitely?"

Her sister pounded a little harder on the dough she was working on the table. "Auntie Mary and I decided to take a break this year while we figure things out."

She gave a meaningful look to her son. "And speaking of Mary—Barrett, go find her. I think she went into her room earlier to do some knitting."

"You mean to take a nap," he said with a grin as he headed out of the room.

"A nap?" she asked as soon as her nephew was out of earshot. The idea of her vibrant aunt taking a nap was as foreign to her as she imagined Couscous Friday—a Moroccan cultural tradition—would be to her family.

"She takes a nap just about every afternoon. She starts in with watching a television show and usually dozes off in the middle of it for a few minutes. Don't forget, she's in her seventies and not as energetic as she used to be, especially since Uncle Claude died."

Hope hated thinking of her aunt slowing down. Mary was her aunt by marriage, wed to the girls' father's oldest brother. She and her husband had become the only thing they had to parents after their parents' tragic deaths only a few months apart.

"You're telling me she wants to close the ranch, too?"

"Celeste voted, too. It was a mutual decision. We didn't have much of a choice."

"But people around here love it. It's as much a tradition as the giant Christmas tree in the town square and the ice rink on the tennis courts behind city hall."

"You think I don't know how much people love the place? I completely get it. This is my home, re- member? You haven't been around since you gradu- ated from high school and left for your study abroad in Europe."

Though she didn't think her sister meant the words as a barb, they stuck sharply anyway.

"But the Ranch is hemorrhaging money, sis. Money we just don't have. Last year it was the stu- pid motor on the rope tow that had to be replaced, the year before that the roof on St. Nicholas lodge. The liability insurance alone is killing us."

Hope frowned. "But Travis loved it. You know he did. Uncle Claude loved it! It was his life's work. He loved everything about Christmas and found the greatest delight in his life by helping everyone else celebrate the holidays. How can you just close the door on all that tradition?"

"Uncle Claude is gone now. So is *Tr-Travis*." Her voice wobbled a little on her husband's name and Hope felt small and selfish for pushing her about The Christmas Ranch.

"It's just me, Mary and Celeste—and Mary isn't as young as she used to be and Celeste works fifty-hours a week at the library in town. That leaves mostly me and it's all I can do to keep the cattle part of the Star N functioning without Travis. We wouldn't have survived harvest and round-up if Chase Bran- non hadn't stepped in to help us and sent a couple of his guys on semipermanent loan, but he's got his own ranch to run."

"I'm here now. I can help. I *want* to help."

"For how long this time?"

The question was a legitimate one. Hope didn't know how to answer. She had finished her teaching obligation in Morocco and had been actively looking around for another one, but at this point her plans were nebulous at best.

"I don't have anything scheduled. I can stay through the holidays. Let me run The Christmas Ranch. You can focus on the cattle side of things at the Star N and I'll take care of everything on the holiday side."

If she thought her sister would jump at the chance for the help, she would have been disappointed. Faith only shook her head. "You don't know what you're saying. It's more than just wearing an elf costume and taking tickets. You haven't been here during the season in years, not since Claude expanded the operations. You've got no experience."

"Except for the five years I spent helping out when I was a kid, when we all pitched in. Those were magical times, Faith."

Her sister's expression indicated she didn't particularly agree. Faith had never much liked the Christmas village, Hope suddenly remembered.

When they had come to Cold Creek Canyon and the Star N to live with Mary and Claude so long ago, they had all been traumatized and heartbroken. Three lost young girls.

Their father had died on Christmas day. The next year, Claude had put them all to work in the concessions stand at what was then only the reindeer petting zoo and the Christmas village with the moving figures. Her older sister had been reluctant to help, and never really wanted much of anything to do with it. She had only agreed after Claude had continued to hint how much he needed her help, in that gentle way of his.

No wonder she had been so quick to close the attraction at the first opportunity.

"Well, *I* thought they were magical times. I love The Christmas Ranch. I can make a success of it, I swear."

"You have no idea what you're talking about. Thanksgiving is next week. There's simply no time to get everything ready in a week and a half!"

She didn't know why this was so important to her but she couldn't bear the idea of no Christmas Ranch. Only at this very moment did she realize how much she had been looking forward to it this year.

She opened her mouth to say so but a flurry of movement in the doorway distracted her. Her aunt appeared, with Barrett close behind.

Her heart squeezed when she saw that it did, indeed, look as if Mary had been napping. The graying, old-fashioned bun she always wore was lopsided and her eyes were still a little bleary. Still, they lit up when they saw her.

"Oh, Hope, my darling! What a wonderful surprise!"

Mary opened her plump arms and Hope sagged into them. This. She hadn't realized how very much she needed the steady love of her family until right this moment.

She could smell the flowery, powdery scent of her

aunt's White Shoulders perfume and it brought back a flood of memories.

"Why didn't you call us, my dear?" Mary asked. "Someone could have driven to the airport to pick you up. Even one of Chase's ranch hands. Did you fly into Jackson Hole or Idaho Falls?"

"I actually flew into Salt Lake City last night and bought a pickup truck near a hotel by the airport. I figured I would need some kind of four-wheel-drive transportation while I was here anyway and I didn't know if you had any extra vehicles around the ranch."

"We could have found something for you, I'm sure. But what's done is done."

Hope didn't mention the noisy engine or the fact that it now was missing most of the passenger-side window.

She made a mental note to find some plastic she could tape up to keep the elements out until she could take it somewhere in town to have the window replaced.

"How long are you staying?"

"I haven't decided yet. Fae and I were just talking about that. What would you say if I told you I would like to run The Christmas Ranch this year."

For just an instant, shock and delight flashed in her aunt's warm brown eyes, then Mary glanced at Faith. Her expression quickly shifted. "Oh. Oh, my. I'm not sure that's a good idea. I don't think you have any idea how much work it is, honey."

She had lived on her own all over the world. She could do hard things—and maybe it was time her family accepted that.

"I know it will be, but I can handle it, I promise. You won't even have to lift a finger. I'll do all of it."

"But, my dear. The reindeer. The sleigh rides. It's too much work for you."

The reality *was* daunting. A tiny little voice of doubt whispered that she didn't have the first idea what she was getting into but Hope pressed it down. This was suddenly of vital importance to her. She *had* to open the ranch. It was a matter of family pride—and belief in herself, too.

"I'll figure something out. I might not be able to do everything, but even a limited opening is better than nothing. Please. Just let me do this. It's important to me. I have such wonderful memories of The Christmas Ranch, just like everyone in town who has been coming here for years."

Aunt Mary was plainly wavering—and in the long run, the Star N was still her ranch and she ought to have final say. Her aunt glanced at Faith, who was pounding the pizza dough so hard it would be a miracle if she didn't pummel all the gluten right out of it.

"The decision to cancel the whole season *was* a huge disappointment, and not just to me," Mary admitted. "You wouldn't believe the comments I've been getting in town."

Hope decided to press her advantage. "It's our civic duty to keep it open this year, don't you agree? Why, it wouldn't be the holidays in Pine Gulch without The Christmas Ranch."

"Don't go overboard," Faith muttered.

"Please. Just give me the chance. I won't let you down."

She could see her sister was wavering. Faith let

out a deep sigh just as her niece Louisa skipped into the kitchen.

"Mom, there's a strange pickup in the driveway. It's kind of junky," she said, then stopped when she spotted Hope.

"Aunt Hope! Hi!"

"That's my junky pickup in the driveway. I'll move it."

"What are you doing here?" her niece asked as she gave her a big hug.

"Guess what? She's going to run The Christmas Ranch!" Barrett exclaimed. "We're going to open after all!"

"Really?" Louisa exclaimed. "Oh, that would be wonderful!"

"We haven't decided that yet," Faith said firmly. "Children, go wash up for dinner and then you can set the table. I'm about to throw the pizza in. Aunt Celeste will be home any minute and we can eat."

"I'm so glad you're home," Louisa said with another hug.

At least a *few* members of her family were happy to see her. Celeste wasn't here yet but she and her younger sister had always been close—of course, she thought she and *Faith* were close, yet her older sister fairly radiated disapproval and frustration.

As soon as the children left the room, Hope suddenly realized her sister wasn't just frustrated. She was angry.

Hope again felt small and selfish. If she were in Faith's shoes, she would be furious, too. Her sister was doing her best to keep the family together. She was managing the ranch, taking care of her children, trying to keep everything running while still reeling from her husband's death.

Now Hope came in and expected to shake everything up and do things her way.

"There is no money, Hope. Do you not get that? You'll have virtually *no* operating budget. You'll barely make enough to pay the salaries for Santa Claus and anybody you hire to work in the gift shop."

Oh. Right. How was she going to find people to help her in only nine days?

Mary could help line her up with the seasonal employees who had worked at the Ranch in previous years. Surely a few of them might still be looking for work.

"You said it's been hemorrhaging money. Is it really that bad?"

"People just aren't coming to holiday attractions like this one much anymore. The only reason we kept it going was because Uncle Claude loved it so and Travis wanted to honor his memory."

Her sister's words were sobering.

"You've always been enthusiastic about things, Hope. It's one of the best things about you. You jump right in and try to fix things. But you can't fix this. The Christmas Ranch is a losing proposition. We just can't afford it anymore. There's no money. We're holding on by our fingernails as it is. If things don't pick up, we're going to have to sell off part of the cattle herd and possibly some of the pasture land along the creek. Wade Dalton made us a more than fair offer and Mary and I are seriously considering it."

"Oh, Faith. I'm sorry. I didn't know."

"I didn't know the whole picture either, until after

Travis died. He was very good at putting on a cheerful face."

Faith was quiet for a moment, then walked around the island. "I should probably tell you, I had a very respectable offer for the reindeer. A guy with a petting zoo in Pocatello. We've talked about it and were planning to take that, too. He was interested in taking them before the holidays."

The small herd of reindeer had been part of the ranch as long as she had lived here. They were part of the family, as far as Hope was concerned.

"Sell the reindeer?"

"I know," Mary piped in. "It breaks my heart too."

"Did you sign any papers?"

"No, but..."

"Don't. Please, Faith. Wait until after Christmas. Give me this season to prove I can turn things around. I know I can do it. I am going to make money with The Christmas Ranch this year, enough to tide the Star N over the rest of the year. You'll see."

Her sister sighed. "You have no idea what you're up against."

"Maybe not, but that could be a good thing, right? Ignorance is bliss, and all that."

"Oh, Hope. You always could talk me into anything."

Mary gave a short laugh. "That's my girls!"

Relief and excitement and no small amount of nerves washed over Hope like an avalanche. "You won't be sorry. This is going to be our best year ever, I promise."

She had no idea how she would keep that promise but she intended to try.

Chapter Three

He was so not cut out for this.

Rafe tried to scrape up the burned bits of the red sauce from the bottom of the saucepan with a wooden spoon but that only mixed the blackened remains into the rest of the mix.

Apparently he would now have to open a bottle of store-bought spaghetti sauce, which is what he should have done in the first place instead of hunting down ingredients then measuring, pouring and mixing for the past fifteen minutes.

Joey wouldn't care if his spaghetti sauce came from a jar. He probably wouldn't even be able to taste the difference.

Rafe headed to the sink and poured the concoction down the sink. There went twenty minutes of his life he wouldn't get back.

Rafe didn't mind cooking. He really didn't. Okay, he didn't mind *grilling*. Apparently there was a difference between throwing a couple of steaks on the old Char-Broil and concocting something nutritious that a seven-year-old kid would actually eat.

He had decided they couldn't live on brats, burgers and take-out alone so had decided to try his hand at a few other things—including spaghetti, which Joey had admitted was one of his favorites.

Now his nephew was due home from his playdate in a half hour and Rafe would have to start over.

Playdates were yet another activity that seemed completely out of his understanding. Give him a terrorist cell and a clear-cut objective to take them out and he could kick some serious ass but apparently he wasn't capable of navigating the complicated politics of playdates—who was allowed to play where, whose turn it was to host, which friends weren't allowed to come over on certain days of the week and which couldn't play at all until their homework was finished.

Truth to tell, the whole parenting thing from soup to nuts scared the he—er, *heck* out of him. What did he know about seven-year-old boys? He could barely remember even *being* one.

He would just have to figure things out. His nephew needed him and he couldn't let him down like he had Cami.

He couldn't let the kid go into foster care. He and his sister had gone the rounds with that, being bounced around between their grandmother, their aunt and finally foster care after their mother's death.

Sure, there were really good foster families out

there. They had been lucky enough to have placement with a few, but he wasn't willing to roll the dice with his nephew's well-being.

Right now, though, he couldn't help but wonder if the boy might be better off taking his chances in the system. Joey might think so. They weren't exactly hitting it off. Rafe never expected to come in like some kind of white knight and save the day but he thought Joey at least might be a *little* grateful to be living with family instead of strangers.

In truth, Rafe was connected by blood to the boy but that was about it. They had lived separately. He had usually been stationed far away from where Cami lived in her wandering life and his relationship with the boy had been mostly through phone calls and emails and the occasional visit.

He supposed he shouldn't be that surprised that trying to establish a normal parental-type relationship with him would be a struggle.

He wasn't sure why the past few weeks had seemed so tough—maybe because he felt out of his element here in this community where he didn't know anybody and didn't have anything else to focus on. Perhaps things would go more smoothly after they returned to California and he figured out what he was going to do now that his whole life wasn't defined by being a navy SEAL.

On the surface, he and Joey should be tight. He had been in the kid's situation when he was young, lost and afraid with no safe harbor. The only difference was that Rafe had had a little sister to worry about, too.

He could completely relate to his nephew's stress and uncertainty that resulted in behavior issues.

His mother had been wild and troubled—giving birth to two children from two different men, neither of whom had stayed in the picture long.

She would clean up her act and regain custody of them for a few months and then something would happen—an unexpected bill, a bad date, even somebody making an offhand comment in the grocery store—and she would fall off the wagon again. All her hard work toward sobriety would disintegrate and they would end up with their elderly grandmother or their aunt, who had been busy with her own family and a husband who hadn't wanted the burden of two more mouths to feed.

A boy should never have to deal with the burden of his mother letting him down, time after time.

More than anything, he wished he could spare Joey that. Since it wasn't possible, he would do his best to provide the kid a stable home environment while his sister was in prison—and if that meant trying to figure out how to provide nutritious meals without burning them, he would do it.

He opened the cupboard and was looking for the bottle of spaghetti sauce he knew he had purchased earlier in the week when the doorbell suddenly rang.

Oh, yay. Maybe when he wasn't paying attention, his subconscious had called for pizza delivery.

He headed to the kitchen and opened the door, only to find someone else unexpected.

It was *her*. The blond and lovely Hope Nichols, who dredged up all kinds of disastrous memories he had buried a long time ago—and who made him feel even more lousy at this whole parenting thing than he already did.

She beamed at him, disconcertingly chipper. "Hi. It's Rafe, right?"

He felt big and stupid and awkward next to all her soft and delicate prettiness. "That's right. Rafe Santiago."

She was probably here to give him the bill for the broken window. What other reason would she have for showing up at his doorstep on a Tuesday evening?

"May I come in? It's freezing out here. My body still hasn't acclimated from the desert."

"Oh. Yeah. Of course. Come in."

He held the door open, kicking aside the backpack Joey had dropped after school that afternoon.

She sniffed and blinked a few times. "Wow. That's...strong."

The house—which was clean and warm but not very homey otherwise—smelled like charred red sauce, he suddenly realized with chagrin.

"Kitchen mishap," he said, embarrassed. "I was making spaghetti sauce and forgot to stir. I just tossed it out but I'm afraid the smell tends to linger."

She gave him a sympathetic look. "Been there, more times than I can count. I'm a lousy cook."

"We could start a club."

She grinned. "Except we'll be very clear that our members are *not* to bring refreshments to meetings."

He couldn't help smiling back. "Definitely. We'll put it in the bylaws."

She paused, then tilted her head. "Do you need a little help? Maybe it's like grammar, you know? Two negatives making a positive. Maybe with two lousy cooks working together, we can come up with something a little more than halfway decent."

"English and math in one paragraph. You must be a teacher."

"Well, I have dual degrees in art history and education. I should also add that while I couldn't bake a decent chocolate cake if cannibals were waiting to nibble off my arms if I didn't deliver the goods, I do make a kick-ass red sauce."

Was she really offering to help him fix dinner? Okay, that was unexpected...and a little surreal.

He ought to politely thank her for the offer and send her on her way. He really wasn't in the mood for the messy conversation about her parents he knew they needed to have—but he had also spent the past few weeks with very little adult interaction and he was a little desperate to talk about something besides Star Wars and Ninjago.

"Couldn't hurt. Between the two of us, maybe we could come up with something Joey might actually eat. So far, my efforts in that direction have fallen pretty flat."

"Excellent. Let's do it." She reached to untwist her multicolored scarf then unbuttoned her red wool peacoat. Beneath, she wore a bright blue sweater that matched her eyes. She looked bright and fresh and just about the prettiest thing he had ever seen.

After an awkward moment, he reached to help her out of it, with manners he had forced himself to learn after he joined the military.

Up close, she smelled delicious, some kind of exotic scent of cinnamon and almonds, and she was warm and enticing.

He told himself that little kick in his gut was only hunger.

He took the coat and hung it on the rack then led the way into the kitchen. "Where do we start?" he asked.

She paused in the middle of the kitchen. "First things first. If you don't mind, I'll just rinse out the rest of this saucepan before the fumes singe away more of my nasal lining."

"Go ahead."

She headed to the sink and ran water in the sink to flush it down then started opening cupboards and pulling things out. "So where is the little snowball-throwing champion?"

"Next door. Playdate with his partner in crime."

"Is this the infamous Samantha?"

"The very same. Last night we had a talk with her and her parents about the dangers of throwing snowballs at cars. It should now be safe to drive through the neighborhood."

"Whew. That's a relief." She started mixing things in the now-clean saucepan. "So what's the story here, if you don't mind me asking? Where are Joey's parents? I would love to hear they're on an extended cruise to the Bahamas and you're just substituting in the parental department for a few days."

His mouth tightened. "I wish it were that straight-forward."

It really wasn't her business but the truth was, he didn't have anybody else to talk to about the situation and found he wanted to explain to her.

"Joe's dad took off before he was born, from what

I understand. I don't know the details. I was overseas."

"Military?"

"How did you know?"

"The haircut sort of gives it away. Let me guess. Marines."

"Close. Navy."

For reasons he didn't want to look at too closely, he didn't mention he had been a SEAL. It was a snap decision—similar to allowing her into his house and his kitchen. If he mentioned it, she might more easily make the connection between him and that rebel camp in Colombia and he couldn't see any good reason to dredge up the painful past they shared while they seemed to be getting along so well.

"Ah. A sailor." She seemed to accept that with equanimity. "So Joey's dad isn't in the picture. What about his mom?"

He pulled a large pot out to boil water for the pasta. Again, he debated what to tell her and then decided to be straightforward about this, at least. "It's a rough situation. My sister is in trouble with the law. She's in jail."

"Oh, no!"

He could have left it at that but he was compelled to explain further. "Last week she pleaded guilty to a multitude of drug charges, including distribution to a minor. Multiple minors, actually. Right now she is in the county jail in Pine Gulch while she awaits sentencing."

"I'm so sorry."

"It's a mess," he agreed.

"So you stepped up to help with Joey."

"Somebody had to. We don't have any other family."

She mulled that as she opened a can of tomatoes and poured the contents into the saucepan. "Are you on leave, then?"

"I had my twenty years in so I retired."

It had been the toughest decision of his life, too, but he didn't add that.

"You gave up your career to take care of your nephew?"

He shifted, uncomfortable. "I'm not quite that noble. I'd been thinking about leaving for a while." That was somewhat true. As he headed into the tail end of his thirties, he had started to wonder if he still had the chops for what was basically a younger man's game. He had started to wonder what else might be out there, but he hadn't been ready to walk away quite yet and had all but committed to re-up for another four years, at least. Everything changed after that phone call from Cami.

"So what will you do now? Are you sticking around Pine Gulch?"

"Only until my sister's sentencing. I'd like to go back to the San Diego area where I have a condo and a couple of job offers, but she begged me to stay until she is sentenced so she can see her son once or twice. I figured it wouldn't hurt to let Joey finish school here since he has friends and seems to be doing okay."

"San Diego is nice. Pretty beaches, great weather. An excellent place to raise children."

He let out a breath, more uneasy at her words than he should be. He was now raising a child. How the he—er, heck was he supposed to do that? The past few weeks had been tough enough. Looking ahead at months and possibly years of being responsible for a boy who wanted little to do with him was more daunting than his first few weeks of BUD/S training.

He would get through this new challenge like he did that hellish experience, by keeping his gaze focused only on the next minute and then the one after that and the one after that.

Right now, the next minute was filled with a beautiful woman in his kitchen, moving from counter to stove to refrigerator with a graceful economy of movement he found extremely appealing. He liked having her here in the kitchen, entirely too much.

Something about her delicate features, the pretty blue eyes and those wild blond curls held back in a ponytail, made his mouth water more than the delicious aromas now wafting from the saucepan she was stirring on the stove.

He wasn't sure he liked this edgy feeling. As a rule, he tended to favor control, order.

His turbulent childhood probably had something to do with his need for calm. He had a feeling Hope was part of it, too—after the way he had screwed up on his very first mission as a SEAL, he had channeled all his guilt and regret into becoming a highly trained, totally focused, hard-as-titanium special warfare operator.

His platoon members called him *Frío*, the Spanish word for cold. Not because he was unfriendly or unfeeling but because he generally turned to ice under pressure.

Come to think of it, that need for order might

be one of the reasons he and Joey were struggling to find their way together. Seven-year-old boys— especially troubled, unhappy seven-year-old boys— tended to generate chaos in their wake.

He'd need to find a little of that ice water in his veins pronto and remember he had enough to deal with right now without this unexpected and unwelcome attraction to someone who would likely hate him if she knew who he truly was.

She hadn't been lying when she said she wasn't much of a cook, but maybe she had exaggerated a little.

She wasn't *terrible* exactly, she just generally didn't have the patience or time for it. There was something quite satisfying about having one specialty, though, and she could say without false modesty that her red sauce was something truly remarkable.

Rafe Santiago and his nephew were in for a treat— if she could relax enough to finish the job while the man glowered at her from his position leaning against the counter next to the sink.

Why did he seem so familiar? She wished she could place him. It could just be that she had encountered more than her share of big, tough military types.

Usually they turned her off. She tended to gravitate toward scholars and artists, not big hulking dudes with biceps the size of basketballs.

The truth was, Rafe Santiago made her nervous and it was a feeling she was completely unaccustomed to.

She forced away the feeling and focused instead on the red sauce. She gave the pot a stir and then grabbed a clean spoon so she could taste it.

"Mmm. Needs more oregano." She shook in a little more and stirred a few more times then grabbed another clean spoon to taste again. "There it is. Perfect. See for yourself."

"I trust you."

"Come on. Try it." She held out yet another spoon for him. After a moment, he rolled his eyes then leaned in and wrapped that very sexy mouth around the spoon.

"Right?" she pushed.

He gave a small laugh that held no small amount of appreciation. "Wow. That is much better than anything I could have come up with."

"Again, to be clear, a good red sauce is literally one of my very few skills in the kitchen. My aunt Mary despaired of me ever learning to even scramble an egg. I have conquered a halfway decent omelet and the red sauce, but that's about it. Oh, and couscous. I just spent three years in Morocco and you can't leave the country without at least trying to make tagines and couscous."

"In the space of five minutes, you've gone from starting a club for people who are helpless in the kitchen to spouting culinary words I barely even know."

"A tagine is both a cooking implement and a dish. Sort of like the word *casserole*. It's a pot that comes with a domed lid. Tagines are also very delicious meat and vegetable dishes, kind of like a stew.

I make a really delicious one with honeyed lemons and lamb."

"Sounds delicious."

"Maybe I'll make it for you sometime."

As soon as the words escaped her mouth, she wanted to yank them back. Why on earth would she say that? She wasn't going to be cooking for the man again. She shouldn't be here now. She had a million other things to do at the moment and none of them had anything to do with fixing a red sauce for Rafe Santiago, even if she was incredibly drawn to the man.

How could she help it, when he talked about giving up his military career to rescue his nephew? It was a wonder she hadn't melted into a mushy pile of hormones on his kitchen floor.

"So what time will Joey be back?"

He glanced at the clock on the microwave.

"Hard to say. I told him five-thirty. So far obeying the rules doesn't seem to be one of his strengths."

She smiled a little at his disgruntled tone. "Well, you'll want to give the red sauce about fifteen minutes more than that, stirring every few minutes. Don't forget to stir. Seriously. Don't forget! I always set a timer to remind me every two or three minutes. If you start your pasta water boiling now, you can add it just as Joey gets back."

"That's it? You come in, throw together dinner and then just take off? You could at least stay and eat it with us."

Oh, she was tempted. If circumstances had been different, she would have jumped at the chance. But, again, she had a million things to do and she couldn't afford any distractions. Rafe Santiago was the very definition of the word *distraction*.

"Sorry, but I can't."

He gave her a challenging sort of look. "Why not? That would at least give you a chance to finally bring up the reason you came here in the first place."

She laughed. "Ulterior motive? Me? Why, you suspicious man. You mean I can't convince you I stopped by just to save you from certain culinary disaster?"

"Yeah, sorry. Not buying it, though I won't complain about the pleasant secondary outcome."

Oh, she liked this man. Entirely too much. Again, she thought how familiar he seemed and was vexed that she couldn't place him.

"All right. You caught me. The truth is, I found an excellent way for Joey to work off the cost of replacing my truck window."

"I suspected as much."

"Okay, here's the skinny. I know you're not from Pine Gulch but are you at all familiar with The Christmas Ranch?"

"Don't think so."

"Well, let me just tell you, sailor, it's a magical place near the mouth of Cold Creek Canyon. My uncle and aunt started it years ago, shortly after they were married. Christmas is kind of a big deal in my family. My family name, Nichols, used to be Nicholas. As in St. Nicholas. You know, the big guy in the red suit with the beard. It was shortened when my ancestors migrated to America several generations ago. Despite that, my uncle Claude and aunt Mary always took the whole holiday thing very seriously."

"Makes sense."

"In spring, summer and fall, the Star N is like any other working cattle ranch, with a pretty small herd but enough to get by. But from Thanksgiving to just after the New Year, an entire section of the ranch is set aside to celebrate Christmas. We have a huge holiday light display, sleigh rides, a sledding hill, even a reindeer petting zoo."

He raised a dark eyebrow. "With real reindeer?"

"You guessed it. We have a herd of ten."

He looked puzzled. "Ten? I thought there were only eight who pulled the big guy's sleigh. Oh, right. You can't forget Rudolph. But then who's the other one?"

"We do have a Rudolph, only we call him Rudy and he doesn't have a red nose except when we stick one on him, which he hates. We've got a bunch more. Glacier and Floe, Aurora and Borealis—we call him Boris for short—Brooks and Kenai and Moraine. Oh, and I can't forget Twinkle and of course Sparkle. He's kind of our favorite. He's the smallest one in the herd and also the sweetest."

"Okay. And you're telling me all this why?"

"It's kind of a long story. Stir the sauce while I tell you."

He made a small, amused sound at her deliberately bossy tone but headed for the stove anyway and picked up the spoon. She tried not to notice how gorgeous he looked doing it.

"My oldest sister and her husband had been running the Star N for the past few years—that's the cattle operation—along with The Christmas Ranch, but Travis was killed in a ranch accident this summer."

"Oh. I'm sorry."

She accepted his condolences with a nod, feeling a sharp ache in her chest all over again. Travis had been her friend and she had loved him from the time he came to live with Mary and Claude to help them run the ranch. She would always miss him but she grieved most that her sister had lost her husband and Barrett and Louisa their father.

"Faith—my sister—is understandably overwhelmed. She's hardly had time to grieve and so she and my aunt Mary and my sister Celeste all decided to take a break from operating the holiday side of things. Since I'm here now and don't have anything going, I offered to take over and run The Christmas Ranch this year. As you can imagine, I have a gazillion things to do if we're going to open in little more than a week. That's where I need Joey's help."

"I hate to break it to you, but I don't think he knows anything about reindeer."

She made a face. "He won't need to deal with the reindeer unless he wants to. But I could really use him after school helping me get everything ready in time for our traditional opening the day after Thanksgiving."

Ten days. She had no idea how she would accomplish the tiniest fraction of what she had to do but she had to start somewhere.

"If Joey can help me every day after school for a few hours that should make us square on the three hundred dollars it's going to take to replace my truck window."

"It would be far easier for me to just pay you the three hundred dollars now and be done with it."

She made a face. "You're absolutely right. But raising boys into men isn't about the easy. It's about consequences and accountability. What lesson would he learn if you stepped in to fix his problem for him?"

"Yeah, yeah. I know. Fine. I'll bring him out tomorrow after school. You said it's in Cold Creek Canyon?"

"Yes. You know where that is?"

"Yes."

"Great. I'll see you tomorrow afternoon, then. Thanks. Have him wear boots and warm clothes. And don't worry. I'll find something fun for him to do."

"Sure you don't want to stay for dinner? Seems only fair, after you did all the work."

She was extraordinarily tempted. She liked the man, entirely too much, but the hard reality was, she didn't have a minute to spare. Even the fifteen minutes she had spent here already was too much.

"I appreciate the invitation and I really wish I could, but I'm afraid I'm going to have to pass."

"I think you're just chicken your sauce won't be edible after all, for all your big talk."

She gave a short laugh. "Wait and see, sailor. Wait and see. Bring that cute nephew of yours over after school, whenever he's done with homework. We're on the north side of the road, about three miles up the canyon. You can't miss it. There's a sign over the driveway that says The Christmas Ranch."

"I'll figure it out."

"Great. See you then."

He started to walk her to the door but she shook her head. "I can find my way out. You need to stay and stir that sauce."

And she needed to do her best to figure out how she was going to keep from losing her head over a man with hazel eyes, a sweet smile and shoulders made for taking on a woman's cares.

Chapter Four

By the time she finally made it back to the Star N, spaghetti with Rafe Santiago and his nephew sounded like the most delicious thing she could imagine, even if the man somehow ended up burning the sauce again.

She was exhausted and starving and trying not to feel completely defeated at the magnitude of the task ahead of her.

Nothing seemed to be going the way she planned. Of their six regular temp employees in years past, three were unavailable or had already found other positions for the season and one had moved away. Only two of their regulars were available to help this year—Mac Palmer, who had been their Santa Claus for years, and Linda Smithson, who helped out in the gift shop.

She was glad to find workers where she could, at least, but she would definitely need to find extra help—in a town she hadn't lived in with any regularity in a decade. It was an overwhelming undertaking.

She was most concerned after her last conversation with Dale Williams. The retired schoolteacher had been their general handyman for a decade and also stepped in to play Santa Claus sometimes, trading off with Mac when needed. But he had had bypass surgery just three weeks earlier and wouldn't be in any shape to help her this year.

She faced the most uphill of uphill battles. A truly epic vertical slope.

While she was tempted to throw in the towel now, before she even started, she absolutely refused.

This might not be the most memorable holiday season The Christmas Ranch had ever enjoyed but she was going to make darn certain it was still a good one.

She repeated the mantra that helped her through the jitters she always had when taking a new teaching job. She could handle this. Heaven knows, she had faced tougher obstacles before.

She and her sisters had survived being kidnapped with their parents by leftist rebels in a foreign country—being held for several weeks in very tiny rooms with no running water and a bucket for a toilet, watching her mother growing increasingly sicker from the cancer ravaging her body while they were helpless to get her the medical help she needed, watching her father die in front of her just when they all thought they would be rescued, then losing her grief-stricken mother just a few months later.

She was a survivor, just like Faith and Celeste. They had found a home here, a true haven after their wandering childhood, and The Christmas Ranch was a big part of that.

She intended to carry on the proud tradition of the ranch and refused to admit defeat simply because she encountered a few obstacles.

She pulled into the circular driveway of the Star N, with its big front porch and the river rock fireplace climbing the side.

She loved this place. No matter where she wandered, from her tiny apartment overlooking the unearthly blue-painted medina in Chefchauan to the tent in the Sahara where she had taught English to Berber tribesmen for a few months to the raised hut on the beach where she lived in Thailand during her Peace Corps time, this was the home of her heart.

Where would she and her sisters have been without Uncle Claude and Aunt Mary to take them in, to wipe their tears and help them back into a routine and put them to work?

They had been extraordinarily lucky to find a place here. Maybe that's why the idea of Rafe Santiago walking away from his naval career to rescue his nephew touched a chord deep inside her.

The living room was dark when she walked inside and she thought for a moment maybe no one was home, until she heard the low murmur of voices coming from the kitchen. She followed the sound and as she approached, she realized it was her younger sister, Celeste. She was reading a children's story and after only a few words, Hope was enthralled.

"It wasn't anywhere close to the magical Christmas Eve Sparkle had dreamed about during the long spring, summer and fall while his antlers turned velvety and soft. It was so much better. The End."

Silence descended for a few seconds when Celeste finished speaking in her melodious, captivating voice—as if the listeners needed time to absorb and reflect—and then both children cheered and begged to hear the story again.

Hope wanted to cheer, too. She walked the rest of the way into the kitchen and found her younger sister at the table with a computer printout in front of her. "Oh, that was a wonderful story!"

Louisa beamed at her. "I know! It's the best one *ever*. I thought nothing could beat the story last year, when Sparkle saved the Elves' Christmas dinner but this one was even *better*."

"Aunt Celeste wrote it," Barrett exclaimed. "Can you believe it?"

She looked at her younger sister, whose cheeks were pink with embarrassment. Celeste was so pretty but hid her loveliness with long bangs, a pony tail, little makeup and no jewelry.

"I can believe it. Celeste has always been the *best* at telling stories."

"I love all the Sparkle stories. She writes a new one every year but I think this one is my very favorite," Louisa said.

Barrett giggled. "Yes. He's so funny, always getting into trouble. In the stories, Sparkle is the smallest reindeer, too, but he's always the one who saves the day."

She had no idea Celeste was a writer but she shouldn't have been surprised. Her youngest sister had always loved books. During their wandering childhood, Faith had always been happiest if she could find a baby to hold or play with, Hope had always been out playing ball or going on adventures and Celeste was perfectly happy reading and rereading the small collection of books their mother had dragged from village to village.

She suddenly had a random memory she must have suppressed, of Celeste and their father trying to keep their spirits up during those dark days of their captivity—when none of them were certain they would survive and their mother was growing increasingly ill—by taking turns spinning stories about heroes and heroines, talking dragons and playful little mice.

They had been wonderful stories, delightful and captivating. Had Celeste been writing stories in her head all this time?

She suddenly felt as if she barely knew her sister. She had thrown so much energy and time into trying to fill some emptiness inside herself by wandering the world and her family had gone on without her.

"I only heard the last few moments but it's lovely. Charming and sweet, Celeste."

"Thanks," her sister murmured. "I have fun coming up with them."

"Do you read them to the children at the library?"

Celeste was the children's librarian in Pine Gulch— the perfect job for her, Hope had always thought.

"Oh, no. Only to Barrett and Louisa."

"They're our special Christmas tradition," Louisa said. "Every year, we have a new one. Aunt Celeste said some day she might put them all in a book so I can read them when I have children."

Hope suddenly had an idea. A perfectly wonderful idea that made her toes tingle and made her arms beneath her sweater sleeves break out in goose bumps.

"Is that the story?" she asked, gesturing to the computer printout on the table.

"Yes," Celeste said warily. "Why?"

"Do you mind if I borrow it?"

"You want to borrow *Sparkle and the Magic Snowball.*"

"Yes. I'd like to read it when I'm not starving to death and can appreciate it better. You've really got a lovely way with prose—take it from someone who has been teaching the basics of the English language for the past four years."

Celeste looked as if she were trying to decide whether to be flattered or suspicious. She must have decided on the former. "You can keep it. I have the digital file on my computer."

"Thanks." She picked up the story, her mind already whirling with ideas. She saw pictures in her mind, probably not surprising since she was an artist at heart, despite the past few years spent teaching English.

"Go ahead and find something to eat. There's some chicken noodle soup in the refrigerator you can warm up and some of Mary's buttermilk breadsticks there on the counter."

Her stomach growled rather loudly and embarrassingly. Barrett snickered while Louisa tried to hide her smile behind her hand.

"You weren't kidding when you said you were starving to death."

"Apparently not. Where are Faith and Mary?"

"They had a shareholders meeting at the irrigation company. I offered to babysit and was just about to tuck these two into bed."

"I can do it," she offered. She had months and years of bedtimes she had missed to make up for.

Celeste shook her head. "You'd better eat before you fall over. I've got this one. I'm sure you'll have plenty of chances to tuck them in before you leave again. Come on, kids."

The children gave her tight hugs then followed Celeste out of the kitchen.

Hope quickly found the soup, thick and rich and brimming with homemade noodles, and warmed a bowl of it in the microwave. She did her best to reheat the breadsticks in the toaster oven then slid down at the table with dinner and her sister's story.

The second time through was even more enchanting. Possibilities danced through her mind and she sketched a few ideas on the edges of the paper. She was still there, her soup now finished, when Celeste came in sometime later.

"You are a fantastic storyteller," she told her sister.

Celeste looked pleased as she started drying dishes in the rack by the sink and putting them away. "Thanks. I guess it's part of the job description when you're the children's librarian."

"You know what we need? A children's storytime at the St. Nicholas Lodge. You would be perfect! You could dress up as Mrs. Claus instead of Aunt Mary doing it and could tell stories to the children.

We could call it Christmas Tales with Mrs. Claus! I love this."

Celeste fumbled a plate but caught it before it could hit the ground and shatter. "I'm glad *you* love it."

"How could you not love it? It's a brilliant idea, if I do say so myself. When you were reading to the children, I completely missed the first part of the story but it didn't matter. The way you told it, I was still enthralled. You have a gift and should share it with the rest of the town."·

Celeste's mouth tightened into a line and in that moment she looked remarkably like their older sister. After a moment, she set the dish and the towel on the counter and came over to the table and slid into a chair across from Hope. "You know I love you, darling, but this just has to be said. You're not going to be able to pull this off in time. You know that, don't you? The ranch is supposed to open in only ten days and nothing is ready."

The panic threatened to flow over her like lava pouring down the mountainside but she pushed it · back. "Why do you think I can't pull it off?"

"You have no business experience. You don't know the first thing about what goes in to making The Christmas Ranch come together each season."

"Uncle Claude wasn't exactly the world's greatest businessman, either," she pointed out.

"Which is one reason the Star N and The Christmas Ranch are operating in the red."

"I'm going to turn things around. You'll see."

"How? You're so good at chasing dreams, Hope. I admire that about you, I do. But when the season is over, you're just going to take off again, leaving all of us to clean up after you. That's assuming you even last through the season."

Was that how her family saw her? As some flighty, irresponsible gadfly, always chasing after the next thing? Dreams, jobs, opportunities. Boyfriends. She hadn't stuck with much of anything for very long.

"You haven't been here the past few months," Celeste went on before she could respond. "You have no idea how tough things have been on all of us. Travis might have been Faith's husband, the children's father, but he was like a brother to me and Mary considered him like a son."

"I know that. I loved him, too, Celeste."

"Losing him hit us all so hard. Everyone is still reeling. I think Faith has probably cried herself to sleep every night since the accident and the kids try to be so brave but I can tell their little hearts are still shattered."

"Poor things," she murmured.

Coming home for the holidays had been the right decision, she thought. Her family needed her, whether any of them wanted to admit it or not.

"None of us has an ounce of holiday spirit this year. How can we? That's the main reason we decided not to open The Christmas Ranch this year. How are we supposed to help other people feel the magic of Christmas when we aren't feeling it ourselves?"

"You know what Mom and Dad always used to say. When your heart is broken, the best way to heal it is to first mend someone else's."

Celeste gave her a hard look. "And Mom and Dad were so smart, they both ended up dead after dragging their daughters from one godforsaken corner of the world to another."

Hope caught her breath, shocked at the bitterness in Celeste's words. How could she argue, though? It was certainly true enough, just not the entire picture.

"That's one way of looking at it," she said quietly. "I prefer to think that they gave their lives doing something they cared about passionately while trying to make the world a little better place."

"We might have to agree to disagree on that one," Celeste said. "I don't have quite your rosy view of what happened to us. The past isn't the issue here, though. The fact remains that I honestly don't understand how Faith and Mary could agree to let you go forward with this harebrained scheme to open the Ranch after we all decided to take this year off while we figure things out."

"I guess they have a little more faith in me than you do," she retorted.

Her sister's expression softened. "I have faith in you. I love you. You know that. And I admire you more than I can say. I love that you go out into the world to explore and dream and *live*."

"But?"

Celeste sighed. "No buts. I know there's no way I can convince you this is a lousy idea. You always did have to charge into things and figure them out on your own."

It was as close as she was likely to get to her sister's approval and she decided to take it. "Thanks, CeCe." She held up the paper. "By the way, I really did love the story. Would you mind if I worked up a few illustrations to go along with it? I have a friend who owns a printing company in Seattle and I was thinking maybe I could talk to her about putting a rush order on printing a few copies and then we could sell them in the bookstore."

Celeste looked alarmed. "Sell them? No! Absolutely not!"

"Why not?"

"Because I was just messing around, trying to come up with something to make Louisa and Barrett smile."

"You did. It's a wonderful story."

"Not wonderful enough to be in a book!"

"Oh, stop. It's a delightful story. You've a gift, my dear. Louisa said you talked about printing up your stories so she could have them to read to her children eventually, right?"

"Well, yes."

"You're going to have children of your own someday. Think of what a wonderful tradition it would be to read a story to them you wrote yourself."

"That would be lovely," Celeste said. She was obviously wavering as she considered the possibilities, so Hope pushed her advantage.

"I have to see if I can come up with some illustrations first. My art skills are a little rusty so I might not be able to—and then I have to check with my friends who own the printing company."

"So it might not happen?"

Oh, she was determined to make it happen. This story was too adorable not to send out into the world.

"Look at it this way. If we don't sell any in the bookstore, you can always give them to Barrett and Louisa for Christmas."

"I guess that's true."

"Do I have your permission, then?"

Celeste—lucky enough not to be named Charity, thus sparing the sisters that triumvirate of virtues for names—finally nodded.

"Sure. Go ahead. I can always use a few more Christmas presents."

"Excellent. Perfect. This is going to be wonderful, CeCe. You'll see."

Her sister didn't look particularly convinced but Hope didn't mind. Her sister would be thrilled with the finished product. She intended to make sure of it.

Chapter Five

Rafe had survived plenty of miserable places during his twenty years in the military. He had hunted through caves in Afghanistan, parachuted into deep, all-but-impenetrable jungles in Laos and had lived off bugs and snakes for two weeks when his platoon had been cut off from radio contact during a mission in Iraq.

Few of those places had struck him as depressing as this small county jail in Nowhere, Idaho, on a late November day.

It didn't help that he sat in front of his sister, wondering again how in the world she had let things go this far. She used to be so pretty, a little round, with big cheeks and dimples. She was always smiling, he remembered, even when their own family situation hadn't been the greatest.

Now she was thin to the point of gauntness, with

huge circles under her eyes and a three-inch scar down her cheek that was new since he'd seen her eight months ago. She looked hard, worn down by the miles she had walked on tough, thorny roads.

"My attorney is really excellent," she was saying now. "Her name is Rebecca Bowman. She's been very kind. She was the one who told me bluntly that the case against me was so clear-cut, my best chance was a plea deal. Because I agreed to testify against Big Mike, I might be able to get a sentence of two to three years, out in eighteen months. That's better than five to ten, right?"

"Sure."

He didn't add that eighteen months was forever in the mind of a seven-year-old. Cami hadn't been thinking of her son in any of this—not when she hooked up with the son of a bitch bar owner slash drug dealer she had met online.

He hated these visits. Not only did they dredge up tough memories of their mother—who had been in and out of jail when they were kids and had spent her last two years on earth behind bars on drug charges before she died of a brain aneurysm—but they also provided stark evidence of his own failures.

He had tried his best for his sister. He had joined the navy as soon as he could and sent almost every penny back to his aunt, who had reluctantly agreed to take Cami into her home.

Cami had been terribly unhappy there and had gone from a laughing, smiling, rosy-cheeked girl to a quiet, sullen teenager. She told him she didn't like living with their aunt and begged him to get out of the military and come back to find a job closer to home.

He had tried to explain to her that he didn't have many options to make an honest living, with no training and no college education. He was an eighteen-year-old kid who could barely take care of himself, forget about his sister.

The military had seemed the best option to build a better future for both of them, and he consoled himself that the money he was sending back each month had to be making her life a little more comfortable.

He had no idea until Cami told him years later that his aunt's husband had been abusing her in just about every possible way.

He *should* have known. He should have done whatever was necessary to protect her and he had failed—now here she was in jail because another son of a bitch had used her and abused her trust.

"Time's almost up," the guard in the corner announced, and Rafe tried not to feel another layer of guilt at his relief.

"How's my little guy?" Cami asked. "Is he doing his schoolwork and staying out of trouble?"

"He's doing okay on the schoolwork front," he said. After a moment's internal debate, he decided to tell her the rest of it. "He broke a window of a pickup truck the other day by throwing snowballs. He was having some kind of contest with one of his friends to see who could hit the most cars and decided to put a rock in one."

"Oh, no. I hope nobody was hurt."

She hadn't seemed too concerned about hurting innocent people when she dragged her son across the country so she and her lowlife boyfriend could deal drugs out of the back room of his bar.

"Nobody was hurt. It just scared the truck owner. A woman by the name of Hope Nichols. After school lets out today, we're going to her place to help her with a little work and repay the debt."

"Joey will probably hate that."

"Too bad," he said. "He made a poor choice and now he has to do what he can to make amends."

It was a message more about her than about her son and both of them knew it. After a moment, Cami nodded. "You're a good uncle and a good man, Rafael."

He wished he could agree. He saw mostly his mistakes and his weaknesses. He saw a man who had been out saving the world when he should have been home helping his sister keep her life on track.

A man whose error in judgment had ended up in the death of a man he was trying to rescue.

"I wish I could have found a man like you instead of a jerk like Michael Lawrence. I don't know what I was thinking."

He could have answered that she was thinking she wanted some kind of safety and security. Mike Lawrence had been a business owner, running a tavern in Pine Gulch, when they met online. After they had been chatting for a few months, he had somehow sweet-talked her into coming to Idaho to "help him out" at the tavern.

Helping him out had meant selling illegal prescription drugs out of the back room of the bar.

Why his sister hadn't picked up her son and gone back to California the minute she figured out what was going was something he would never understand.

"Time's up," the deputy intoned. "Back to your cell."

Cami stood up, looking small and vulnerable. He hated thinking of her behind bars. He just had to hope she had the strength of spirit to accept the consequences of her own choices better than their mother had.

"Thank you for coming to see me. I know you hate it."

"I hate it," he acknowledged. "But I love you, which makes it a little easier."

Her eyes softened and filled with tears. He wished he could reach out and hug her but physical contact was forbidden.

"Thanks for everything. Give Joey my love, okay?"

He nodded and watched her being led back to her cell, his emotions in tumult. He wanted to pound something. A tree, a concrete wall. He didn't care what.

He walked out of the jail into the pale sunshine, wondering what the hell he was going to do now. Joey wouldn't be home from school for another three hours and he sure as hell didn't feel like going back to that crummy rental house and watching daytime TV.

He climbed into his SUV, tempted to drive to the *other* tavern in town, the Bandito, and have two or three—or ten—beers. Since he made it a point never to drink when he was upset, instead he headed on impulse toward Cold Creek Canyon.

He told himself he was only scoping out the place, doing a little recon to make sure he could find The Christmas Ranch when Joey's school let out.

That didn't quite explain why, when he saw the sign for The Christmas Ranch, where your holiday dreams come true—and a smaller one that read Closed Indefinitely—he found himself turning into the parking lot.

No harm in looking around, he told himself, seeing what might need to be done.

The place looked pretty vacant. He saw a boarded-up lodge-like building with big river rock chimneys on either end and an empty pen next to it with a barn that must be the home for Rudy, Sparkle, Whosy-whatsit and the other reindeer.

The place had a certain charm, he had to admit, but he could see it needed some basic maintenance work. As he climbed out of the SUV, he could see a few sagging shutters, a rain gutter that had come loose, a big hole in the fence.

If she was going to whip this place into shape, she needed some serious help.

He walked around the building, casing the situation like he would gather advance intel for a mission.

The weather had turned warmer, melting off what remained of the few inches of snow they'd had over the weekend. It wasn't quite strip-off-your-coat weather, but the wind didn't have that bitter bite of a few days earlier.

For a moment, he lifted his face to the pale November sun and breathed in air scented with pine and sage. A guy could get used to this, definitely.

He headed around the building, taking note of a few other repairs that needed to be finished. When he returned to his vehicle, he found a familiar old blue pickup truck parked next to his SUV—and a beautiful woman climbing out.

Something in his chest gave a quiet little sigh when he spotted her. He decided not to let that bother him. So he was happy to see her. There was no crime in that.

"Hi! What are you doing here?"

He suddenly found himself wanting to tell her the whole ugly business. About Cami and the ass-hat she got messed up with, about her sentencing—and, further back, about their mother and her complete lack of nurturing.

He pushed away the demons. "I was in the neighborhood," he lied, then decided there was no point in it, since nobody drove into the out-of-the-way box canyon of Cold Creek unless they had a reason to be here.

"Okay, I wasn't in the neighborhood. I drove here on purpose. Call it a recon mission. I wanted to make sure I could find the place later when I need to bring Joey. And since I was already here, I decided to take a look around. Looks like you've got your work cut out for you."

"Funny, sailor. By the looks of you, I never would have guessed you're a master of understatement."

He smiled, his mood suddenly much brighter. She headed around the back of the pickup truck and pulled down the tailgate then reached to tug a ladder out of the bed.

Rafe followed her and took the weight of the ladder from her. "I've got this."

"You don't have to help me. I can handle it."

"You're doing me a favor. I was looking for something physical to do. This fits the bill nicely. Where are we heading with it?"

"Over there." She pointed to the sign above the entrance to the parking lot. "I need to take down the closed sign and let people know we are no longer *closed indefinitely.*"

She pulled another sign out of the pickup bed, a huge painted white sign that read Opening the day after Thanksgiving, and below that, Better than Ever.

In light of all the obstacles she faced, he found her optimism refreshing, a bright spot in an otherwise miserable day.

He carried the ladder back to the entrance and set it up under the other sign.

"Thanks. Thanks a lot." She headed to the bottom of the ladder and set one foot on the first rung from the ground.

"Can you hand me the sign when I go up a few more rungs?" she asked. Her hands suddenly gripped the side of the ladder for dear life and a sudden fine sheen of perspiration had appeared on her top lip. Her hands were shaking, he realized. Despite the obvious signs, it took him a minute to put everything together.

"You don't like heights much, do you?"

She set her foot back on the ground. "How did you guess?"

He wasn't sure she would appreciate knowing her pale face and pinched lips sort of gave things away. Instead, he only smiled again. He had only great admiration for people who were afraid of things but confronted them head-on anyway.

"I must be psychic. Hand over the hammer and the nails. I've got this."

"Oh, but…"

He shook his head. "No worries. I've got no problem with heights. I'm used to jumping out of airplanes or helicopters or boats for that matter."

"No. You don't have to. I can do this."

Yeah, he respected the heck out of that determination in her voice. "So can I. Were you planning on using that hammer in your pocket to adhere the sign? Hand it over, then, and whatever nails you want me to use."

She looked at him and then up at the sign again. Apparently she decided there was no shame in accepting help.

"Fine. Here you go. Knock yourself out."

She reached into the pocket of her jeans and pulled out a handful of nails, still warm from being so close to her body heat, then handed over the hammer. Their hands brushed as she dropped the nails into his palm and he was aware of a little quiver of awareness in his gut.

"So why don't you like heights?" he asked, mostly to distract himself from an attraction he didn't want to feel and wouldn't do anything about anyway.

She shrugged. "I just don't. Never have."

Did it have anything to do with that frantic helicopter ride in Colombia, when she had fought and screamed and tried to jump back out to race toward her father, who was obviously beyond saving at that point?

He could help her, more than just hanging this sign.

As he climbed the ladder and started taking down the other sign, he realized he wanted to try. Helping her get this big worn-down mess ready for the holidays would give him something to fill his days and maybe, in some small way, would help him feel like he had at least tried to make things up to her.

He couldn't do anything for his sister right now, except take care of Joey. But he could take a little burden off the shoulders of Hope Nichols by helping her make this place ready for the season.

He pulled the Closed sign off. "Watch it," he called down before he dropped it to the ground.

"You ready for the new one?" she asked.

"Yes."

He stepped down a few rungs and took the sign she handed up to him. One side was easy. He lined it up in the same holes as the other had been but the new sign was much longer than the other one had been so he had to climb down, move the ladder over to within reach, then climb back up.

He glanced down at her. "Tell me when it's straight."

She tilted her head, looking bright and lovely in the afternoon sun. "A little higher. No, now down just half a hair."

"How's that?" he asked around the nails in his mouth. "Is it straight?"

"Oh, perfect. Absolutely perfect."

He decided to take her word for it as he hammered the nails in then climbed down the ladder.

"There you go."

"Thank you. I'm sorry to be such a big baby. About the height thing, I mean."

He raised an eyebrow. "Did I say you were a baby?

From what I saw, you didn't want to climb that ladder but you were ready to do it anyway. That's the exact opposite of cowardice."

His words obviously surprised her. Head tilted, she studied him much the same way she had the sign, trying to figure out his angle.

He didn't want her looking too closely, wondering at his motives for helping her. "What else can I do? I've got two hours before I need to pick up Joey from school and nothing on my agenda but finding something to fill the time. I noticed a couple shutters loose on the lodge. I'll start there."

"You're not serious."

"Completely. I want to help. You want the truth, I need something to do or I'm going to go crazy. I'm at loose ends right now while Joey is in school, until Cami's sentencing. We won't be here long enough for me to look for a job somewhere and I'm not very good at sitting around watching daytime television. I'm grateful to have something to do—and by the looks of it, you have enough work to keep a dozen of me busy."

"At least," she muttered.

"So what's keeping you from letting me help? I worked in construction here and there while I was in high school and the summer before I joined the navy. I'm not a master carpenter but I can make a straight cut and drive a nail."

She looked at him suspiciously. "I don't understand. Why do you want to help me? If you think you're going to get a huge paycheck, I'm afraid that's not happening. I can pay you, but not much more than minimum wage."

He wanted to tell her she didn't need to pay him anything but he knew that would only make her more suspicious. He couldn't tell her *why* he owed her so he only shook his head.

"I'll help pay off Joey's window debt. After that, you can take the money you would have paid me and donate it to your favorite charity. A school for girls in Afghanistan. Clean drinking water in Guatemala. I've got a buddy who works at a recreational therapy program for injured war veterans outside of Hope's Crossing, Colorado. I can hook you up with him, if you want, and you could donate it there."

He suddenly remembered her family situation. "Or just give it to your sister. You said she lost her husband a few months back. Maybe she can throw a little extra Christmas cheer in her kids' stockings this year."

It was apparently the right thing to say. Her eyes softened and the smile she gave him was as sweet as a summer evening. "Oh. You are a very good man, Rafe Santiago."

This was the second woman who had said that to him in the past hour. He wanted to tell her he was far from good but he wasn't willing to explain all the reasons why.

Instead, he shoved the hammer into the pocket of his jacket and folded up the ladder.

"Show me where to start."

If she had an ounce of sense, she would tell him to move along, that she didn't need his help.

Yes, it would be a lie. She needed his help rather desperately but she didn't *want* to need his help.

This man was dangerous. She didn't mean that in a physical sense. Though he radiated a sense of implacable strength and barely leashed violence—he had probably done very well for himself in the military—she sensed he wouldn't hurt her. Or anyone else in her family, for that matter.

She was incredibly drawn to him and she didn't want to be. For one thing, the timing was horrible with all the other plates she had spinning. For another, he was just too big, too tough, too *male* for her to be at all comfortable entertaining this unwilling attraction.

"I did mention I've only got a few hours before I have to pick up Joey, right?"

With a start, she realized he had asked her a question and was waiting for an answer. How long had she been standing there staring at him?

"Yes. Sorry. My mind, er, wandered." Into areas she had absolutely no intention of sharing with him.

"Any idea where you'd like me to start?" he asked again.

Hope drew in a breath. This was stupid. If she wanted to prove to her sisters she could handle the responsibility for running The Christmas Ranch, she needed to use her brain. She couldn't afford to turn away an offer of help simply because she was too attracted to the man making the offer—especially when he didn't want to take a salary for his work and insisted she donate it to a needy cause instead. How much more perfect could he get?

"If you're sure, the fence around the petting zoo has a few slats that need to be replaced. Once you finish that, we can bring the reindeer over from the other pasture and get them settled in."

She eyed him up and down, trying not to notice the breadth of his shoulders or the way his jacket hugged narrow hips. "You're not really dressed for kneeling in the dirt," she pointed out. "It might be muddy, especially after the uncertain weather of the past few weeks."

"Don't worry about me. I'll be fine," he assured her. "Everything is washable. I even have work gloves in my SUV, believe it or not."

"I appreciate a man who is prepared. I just came back from a trip to the lumberyard and you should find plenty of supplies in the back of my truck. I can drive closer to the pasture to unload it."

"Sounds good."

She climbed back into her truck, grateful again for whatever crazy impulse had prompted her to buy the pickup in Salt Lake City just a few days earlier instead of renting a small compact car for her stay.

Had it really only been a few days since she had landed from Africa? She couldn't believe her life had changed so much in such a short amount of time.

He met her at the pasture after she backed the truck up as close as she could manage, then started unloading the lumber she had purchased to replace the damaged section.

Rafe immediately started tearing off the broken, weather-rotted slats, as if he had done this sort of thing before.

"How does your typical Idaho cattle rancher end up dipping his toes into the reindeer business?" he asked while he worked.

She smiled a little. "I told you how much my uncle Claude loved Christmas. He had a friend in Montana who got a couple of reindeer and talked him into trying it."

She remembered how much her uncle had loved introducing children to the usually docile creatures—starting with his nieces. "My sister wants to sell the reindeer. I don't know how she can. They're like family now."

She felt guilty all over again that she hadn't been here these past few years since Claude died to help with the Star N and The Christmas Ranch. She didn't know whether she could have made any difference in the balance books but she would have liked to try.

"Neither of my sisters wanted me to open the ranch this year. Safe to say, they are both quite opposed to it. I thought we all had wonderful memories of working here, but apparently I was the only one who really enjoyed it. Funny, how individuals can remember the same events very differently, isn't it?"

"I suppose it's all about point of view. We all filter our situations through our own unique lens, which is shaped by our history, personality, experiences."

She nodded at the insight. "Exactly."

"Six guys on the same mission can tell very different stories in the debrief. It's an interesting phenomenon."

She wondered about his background. If he had been in the military for twenty years, she could only imagine the stories he might tell.

She found Rafe an incredibly fascinating man—and not only because she liked how he looked and the way he moved. She couldn't help being intrigued with a man who would give all that up to take care of a seven-year-old kid.

"When you showed up, you said you needed something physical," she said. "Forgive me if I'm jumping to conclusions, but you seemed upset. Is everything okay?"

His hands tightened on the hammer and he may have pounded just a little harder than before but other than that he showed no emotion. "Not really. I just came from the jail, visiting my sister. I try to go a couple times a week."

"Oh, that must be tough. I'm sorry. How is she doing?"

Surprise flickered in his gaze for just a moment, as if he hadn't expected the question.

"She's holding up okay. She knows she's in this mess because of her own choices and that she can't get out of prison time. It's just a matter of how long she'll be in, at this point, and that's entirely up to the judge."

"That must be tough, especially when she has a cute little boy who needs his mom."

"Maybe she should have thought about that before she made a string of really stupid choices that led her where she is."

She might have thought his words cold and unfeeling, if not for the shadows in his gaze and the thread of pain she heard twisting through his tone.

"Your plan is to stick around until her sentencing?"

He hammered a little harder. "Yeah. I can't say I'm not thrilled about it but it makes the most sense. Joey has been doing well in school this year, which is something of a miracle, judging by his past record. The school counselor and principal met with me last week and both suggested it might be best not to start him at a new school until after the Christmas break. Since that coincides with Cami's sentencing a few days before Christmas, I guess that's the plan."

He was silent for a moment. "I haven't really been there for her over the years. I guess the least I can do is stick around right now when she needs a little moral support."

Oh. She could really lose her head over a man like him.

Not that she intended to let herself. On a strictly emotional level, he made her nervous. She liked being in control of most situations, which was probably why she typically dated rather passive men who let her take the lead in their relationships.

She had a feeling Rafe wasn't much of a follower.

Not that she intended to put that theory to the test. She could accept she needed him to help out here at The Christmas Ranch but she simply had no time for a relationship—and certainly not with a man whose personal life was even more tangled than hers right now.

They were done far earlier than she would have expected. "That was quick. You do good work. Maybe you should think about becoming a builder now that you've left your seafaring ways behind."

A muscle worked in his jaw, and she couldn't tell if he wanted to smile or frown at her.

"I've still got an hour before I need to pick up Joey from school and bring him back here. Is there something else I can do in that amount of time?"

"My checklist is longer than Santa's right now. Everything needs attention. This morning, I was thinking the top priority should be probably be the main building. We call it the St. Nicholas Lodge. This is where you'll find the ticket office, the gift shop, the concession stand where we sell hot chocolate and roasted chestnuts, that sort of thing. It used to be an old barn until Uncle Claude fixed it up. That was years ago, right after we came to live on the Star N."

His expression seemed tense suddenly, though she couldn't begin to guess why.

"Things are starting to fall apart inside the building," she went on. "I noticed a few of the tables were wobbly and some of the chairs have lost their legs. The whole place just needs basic attention."

"I picked up the same thing outside when I was walking around earlier. Why don't I do a quick inventory to see what needs to be done inside? Since I'm heading back into town anyway to pick up Joe, we can stop by the hardware store and pick up any other supplies I might need before we head back here?"

She smiled, grateful all over again for his help. Having him on her side helped make the whole undertaking seem a little less daunting. "Excellent. I like a man with a plan."

Something hot and intense flashed in his gaze for only a moment then was gone. Still, just seeing it there sent heat rushing to her cheeks. She knew she must be blushing, the curse of her fair skin.

She turned away, hoping he would think her rising color was from the cool wind that had just picked up and was playing with a stray lock of hair that had fallen from her ponytail. "Come take a look inside.

When you see how much work needs to be done in only nine days from now, you might be sorry you ever offered to help."

Chapter Six

Rafe followed Hope, trying not to notice how well she filled out the soft pair of old blue jeans she wore or the enticing swing of her ponytail that made him want to pull all that wavy tangle of blond hair free and wind it around his fingers.

He needed to remember the reason he was here. He had an obligation to this woman and her sisters dating back seventeen years—an obligation that firmly superceded any inclination he might have to ogle her lush curves.

He followed her into the building, which seemed dark and musty and cold.

She flipped a switch and a couple of big light fixtures made up of entwined elk antlers illuminated and warmed the cavernous space divided into a ticket counter, a small area with display cases that looked like it held old holiday paraphernalia, another area with empty shelves that likely held a gift shop, a large throne-like chair in one corner that was probably Santa's domain and two huge river rock fireplaces that dominated each wall. A massive spruce tree had been set up in one corner but was currently undecorated.

"It's impossible to keep this place warm enough, as you might have guessed. We run both fireplaces during the season and it's still drafty in here, unless the place is packed. The rest of the time, we try to get by with the industrial-size space heaters, which seem to do okay."

Though the space was large, it was quite comfortable and he imagined that children and adults would probably find it very appealing.

"This is nice."

"Thanks. Everything could use a coat of new paint but we don't have time for that. Maybe next year."

Would she still be here the next year? From all she had said about her history, she seemed to like to wander.

"You said the tables are a little wobbly?"

"Yes, and we've got a couple of chairs that somehow lost their legs while they were stored over the summer. Oh, and I noticed the armrest on Santa's chair has come loose."

If someone had told him a month ago that he would find himself in a place called St. Nicholas Lodge in rural Idaho, repairing Santa's chair, he would have called them crazy. His life had taken some really crazy twists and turns over the years but this had to be one of the craziest.

"I'll take a look."

"Great. Thank you. Do you need something to write down what you need in the way of supplies?"

"That wouldn't hurt."

She disappeared for a moment through a door behind the ticket counter and emerged with a pad and pencil. "Here you go. When you're done, find me in the office back there. I'm still in the middle of taking inventory of the gift shop stock left over from last year so I can see what else we need to order."

"Got it."

She disappeared into the office and he wandered through the building, taking note of what needed to be fixed, prioritizing things as he went into columns under *urgent, important* and *long-term.*

When he finished, the list was longer than he expected but most items were things that could wait. He made his way behind the ticket counter and paused for a moment in the doorway, watching her.

Even though they had only been separated for fifteen or twenty minutes, he was taken by surprise all over again by how lovely she was, rather wild and untamed-looking with her stunning blue eyes and that mane of blond curls. He could only imagine what an exotic creature she must have appeared in her travels in Morocco and Thailand.

She was looking at something on the desk and he could tell by the furrows in her forehead and the tension in her shoulders that it upset her.

As far as he could tell, she wasn't crying but she still looked sad. He should leave her alone. She wouldn't appreciate being spied on in a moment of distress. He was about to turn away and head back outside but she sensed his presence and turned before he could escape.

"Oh," she said, her voice a soft exclamation. "Hi."

He cleared his throat. "Everything okay?"

"Yes. Sorry. I just found a picture in a drawer while I was looking for a receipt. It brought back a lot of memories."

He moved closer to stand beside the desk and found an old snapshot of three girls. She and her sisters, he realized. They looked very much like he remembered from that botched rescue. Maybe a little older but not much. They were standing around an older couple, the man in a Santa suit and the woman dressed as Mrs. Santa.

"Cute."

"That's Uncle Claude in the Santa suit and Aunt Mary as Mrs. Santa." She smiled a little. "That was about a year after we came here, when The Christmas Ranch started becoming what it is today. I've never been so busy. I think Claude and Mary purposely gave us a million things to do on the ranch that Christmas so we wouldn't have time to brood. Genius, really."

"Brood about what?" he asked, even though he obviously knew the answer.

"Oh, you know. The first Christmas without our parents. Our dad was killed on Christmas the year before that picture and our mom died of cancer just a few months later."

He should tell her.

The inner voice prompted him loudly that now would be the perfect time but he pushed it away. She didn't need to know he had been there. If she did, she might not let him help and he suddenly found he wanted to, more than he would have believed possible a few hours earlier.

"That's tough," he said in a noncommittal sort of way.

She shrugged. "It could have been worse, believe me. We were okay here and, most important, we were all together. Claude and Mary loved us and did the best they could to show us that. We were lucky, really."

"That doesn't make it any easier."

"No. It doesn't. But nobody's life is perfect, right?" She smiled a little and he was fiercely drawn to her. He gazed down at her, thinking how easy it would be to lean in a little more or, better yet, pull her out of the chair and into his arms.

He drew in a breath, his heartbeat loud in his ears.

At the very last minute, before he would have acted on the insane impulse, he tossed the list in front of her and forced himself to ease away from the desk and from her. "This is what I found that needs to be fixed. It's a pretty long list but many of the things on there aren't necessarily urgent. I figured I would focus on the most important and see how far I get."

"Let's see." She picked up the list. While she perused it, she absently licked her bottom lip and he almost threw his good intentions out the window and kissed her anyway.

"You're right. It's a big list."

"I figure I can knock off many of those things in a few hours of work today or in the morning, especially if I can pick up the supplies now."

She looked worried, suddenly. "Look, I've been

thinking. I appreciate your help but I can't take advantage of you like that."

Go ahead. Take advantage of me, any way you want.

He shook his head. "We've covered this. I've got nothing to do right now. In truth, you're doing me a favor by giving me something to do, so just let it go. Please. And speaking of going, I need to. Joey will be out of school in a few minutes. I'll take him home to change into work clothes and then we'll run to the hardware store before we come back here. I'll see you in an hour or so."

She looked as if she still wanted to argue but he didn't give her a chance; he simply picked up the list from the desk and headed out the door, before he did something really stupid.

Hope waited until he walked out of the office and she heard the outside door to the lodge close before she sank back down into Uncle Claude's chair.

She pressed a hand to her stomach, where an entire ballet troupe of butterflies seemed to be performing the *Nutcracker Suite*.

Had Sexy Navy Man really just almost kissed her? Maybe she had misread the signs—that slight flaring of his pupils, the way he suddenly couldn't seem to take his gaze off her mouth.

Maybe he hadn't wanted to kiss her. Maybe she had a piece of lettuce stuck in her teeth or something.

She wanted to believe that explanation. It would be simpler—though, of course, more embarrassing—than trying to accept the idea that a gorgeous guy like Rafe Santiago might be interested in her.

She drew in a shaky breath, trying to remind herself he wasn't her type. *At. All.*

The few casual boyfriends she had allowed herself over the years in college and then through her time in the Peace Corps and while she was teaching English had been the lean, erudite, scholarly types. Guys who would rather stay up all night discussing philosophy or politics or art than making love.

Something told her Rafe Santiago would *not* be that sort of man.

Not that she had any intentions of finding out. Neither of them had time for this sort of distraction right now. If this happened again, she would have to just be blunt with him and explain she had too much on her plate right now to worry about a sexy sailor with hazel eyes and a broad chest that made a woman think he could bear all her troubles without even blinking…

She drew in a sharp breath and placed her hands on the desk. What was the point in angsting about it for another instant? Good grief, the man hadn't even kissed her. If he had even been considering it, he obviously came to his senses. She would focus on that and be grateful one of them, at least, was thinking clearly.

She turned back to the inventory list just as she heard the outside door to the lodge open.

"Hope? Are you here?" she heard Faith call.

"Yes," she answered. "In the office."

A moment later, her sister poked her head in the doorway. She was wearing a ranch coat, boots and jeans—and a concerned frown.

"Who was that guy I just saw driving away?" she asked. "I didn't recognize the vehicle."

Only the most fascinating man she had met in a long, long time.

"Do you remember I told you about the boy who knocked out my window the day I arrived? He is going to work off his debt to me by helping out around here, since I'm in desperate need. His uncle was just checking out the situation before he brings his nephew out after school. He's offered to help with some of the basic maintenance while we try to whip this place into shape."

Faith gave her a sharp look. "While *you* try, you mean. Keep the rest of us out of this, if you please."

While her sister might have reluctantly agreed to let her open The Christmas Ranch, she had obviously not reconciled herself to the idea completely. She wasn't openly hostile but every time the subject came up, Faith was quick to point out that the struggling cattle side of the ranch took precedence.

Hope adored her older sister and always had, even before the tragic events of that long-ago December. Faith was the strongest person she knew, with a tough resilience that was tempered by soft compassion.

When they moved from place to place as girls as their parents took new missionary assignments, Faith had always been the one to make friends first and to help her younger sisters find their way.

That shared trauma had forged a stronger-than-usual bond between all three of the sisters and Hope regretted this conflict between them.

She held out the old picture from Claude's desk. "Look what I found while I was cleaning today."

Faith moved closer to take a look. "Seems like a lifetime ago," she said. "Look at my hair. What was I thinking, with those huge bangs?"

"I know. I'm the brace-face there. We had fun that season, didn't we? Do you remember how Uncle Claude made us dress up in little elf costumes while we sold concessions and handed out candy canes to the children?"

Faith shuddered. "I remember being so humiliated when friends from school would come out to the Ranch that I would try to hide in the bathroom so they wouldn't see me."

"I remember my friends acting like they were too cool to have fun when they came here but they were always the first ones to go all goo-goo-eyed over the reindeer and always fought each other to be the first one to sit on Santa's lap," Hope said.

She paused. "We were so busy that first Christmas, we didn't really have time to grieve. Don't you think it was good for us to have something to occupy our time and energy when otherwise we might have been sitting home brooding on the anniversary?"

Faith gave her a long, measured look. "Do you really think I don't know where you're going with this? The answer is no."

She leaned back in the chair. "Hmm. Can you be more specific? I don't know what question you thought I was going to ask."

"You want Louisa and Barrett to help you out here."

Faith had always been entirely too perceptive. Hope could never fool her.

"Nothing too strenuous," she assured her. "I

thought they could help me with a few fun jobs like setting up the Christmas village and decorating the tree in here."

"They have enough to do after school with school-work and their chores."

Faith was their mother, Hope reminded herself. She knew best. Still...

"Uncle Claude was a genius. I don't think I fully realized it until today, looking at that picture. Do you really think he wanted to expand The Christmas Ranch that year for his own sake? Or did he do it to keep three grieving girls busy during that first Christmas without our parents?"

"Distraction isn't always the best policy."

"In this case, it worked, didn't it? Think of how lost we would have been without those silly elf costumes, the sleigh rides, the reindeer."

"We were much older than Louisa and Barrett are," she pointed out.

"Yes," Hope acknowledged. "And we had already had nearly a year to go through the grieving process, while they are still only a few months out of losing their father. I know. The situations aren't the same. I just thought helping out here might give them something to look forward to in the afternoons. I'll pay them, of course, and they can use the money for Christmas presents for you and Auntie Mary and Celeste."

Faith didn't look convinced. Perhaps she ought to let it drop. She didn't want to argue with her sister or have one more point of contention between them. Yet when she looked at the picture still in her sister's hand, she couldn't help remembering all the good times they'd had here.

In many ways, working at The Christmas Ranch had shaped their childhood as much as those early years as the children of earnest wandering medical missionaries. It had reinforced to her the magic of Christmas and the joy that could be found in bringing that to others.

"Please, Fae. It will be good for them and I'll make sure they have fun."

Her sister let out a heavy sigh. "Fine. I'll talk to them. If—and only *if*—they want to help after their homework and regular chores, I won't stand in the way."

She beamed and stood up to give Faith an impulsive hug. "Thanks! You know you're the best older sister ever, right?"

Faith snorted but hugged her back. "Cut it out. I already said I would let them help you. You don't have to lay it on any thicker."

Maybe Rafe had changed his mind and decided not to come.

Hope frowned at her watch. It was nearly four-thirty. He had been gone for two hours. Perhaps he had decided he didn't want to become entangled with her crazy plans after all, that she was too much trouble.

No. She couldn't believe that. He had promised and she sensed he was a man of his word. He must have encountered a problem.

Louisa and Barrett hadn't come down from the main house either, but she hadn't expected them yet, with their homework and chores. Meanwhile, it would be full dark by six-thirty, which gave them very little time to accomplish what she had hoped for the evening.

Since the afternoon was moderately warm for November—jacket weather, not parka—she had decided to focus on some of the outside jobs while they had the chance.

Snow was forecast for later in the week and she and the children could decorate the Christmas tree when they were stuck inside. She carried another box and set it on the flatbed wheeled wagon and had just turned to go back into the storage room off the back of the lodge when she heard a vehicle in the parking lot.

A moment later, she saw Rafe climb out of his SUV and open the door to the backseat. Joey hopped out and followed him over to Hope, though she couldn't help notice he was dragging his feet.

"Hi," Rafe said in a harried sort of voice. "Sorry we're late. We had some issues after school with another kid."

Joey lifted his head and she blinked at the truly impressive shiner he had going.

"Oh, honey. What happened?"

"Nothing," the boy muttered. He was so full of pain. It seemed to radiate off him in waves and her heart ached for him. He must be so frightened to be without his mother.

She hated seeing anybody hurting and she wanted to help him, but how could she? She wasn't a counselor or a social worker. She was a stranger brought into his life by accident, who would only be there for a few weeks.

"I'm so glad you're here," she said suddenly. "I really need some help and I think only you can do it."

"Me?" He still looked sullen but she could see a trace of curiosity in his expression, as well.

"Yes. Come on over here, please."

She led the way to the reindeer pen, where she had just finished moving the herd.

He gaped at the animals inside the pen. "Are those real reindeer?"

"They are indeed."

"Are they babies? I thought they would be bigger."

"Lots of people do. Reindeer are actually often smaller than mule deer. Our herd is from a particularly small strain."

"Can they hurt me?"

"They're very gentle, since we have raised them all from very young. They're more like pets. But you don't have to go close to them if you don't want and you should never go near them unless an adult is there, too. Now wait right here and you can help me."

He leaned against the fence Rafe had just fixed while she slipped between the slats and headed for Sparkle, the smallest of the lot. He came to her readily, always friendly and up for fun, and she attached a leadline to the bridle she had already put on him and led him over to where Rafe and Joey watched. She held the line out to him.

"I need you to hold this for me while I go find a friend to help us."

"Me?"

"Yes. Do you think you can do it?"

He looked at Rafe as if for permission. His uncle shrugged and after a moment, Joey reached out and grabbed the line from her. She didn't have to go far to find another reindeer. Twinkle, always curious, had come to see what was going on. Sparkle's sister quickly let her attach a second line and lead her over to Joey.

"All right. Now you see that wagon over there? We're going to hook them up so they can help us today. Just hold on to the lead there and come with me."

"Are you sure this is safe?" Rafe asked.

"Perfectly," she assured him. Joey's sullenness seemed to have disappeared and he looked entranced as he followed her through the gate, leading the sweet and docile Sparkle behind him.

He looked nervous but still absolutely thrilled at the responsibility. At the wagon, he held Sparkle's lead while she harnessed Twinkle and then he stepped away while she did the same for Sparkle.

Just as she was finishing, they were joined by Louisa and Barrett, wearing jeans and cowboys hats.

"Mom says we can help you on The Christmas Ranch!" Louisa said breathlessly, as if she had run all the way down from the main house.

"Did you finish your chores?" Hope pressed.

"Yep. And I didn't have any homework and neither did Barrett."

"I finished my math worksheet in class," Barrett said proudly. "Now all I have to do is read for twenty minutes to Mom and we do that at bedtime, only sometimes she falls asleep before I'm done."

Her heart squeezed for her sister, who was running harder than Hope was, trying to keep the Star N going.

"Excellent job. Homework and chores first, then you can help me. That's the deal I made with your mom."

Louisa made the sort of disgruntled face only a nine-year-old girl could manage. "I know. She said. Only then it will be time for dinner and almost bedtime."

"I have a feeling you'll have plenty of chances to help before Christmas is over," Hope assured her.

Louisa gave Joey a friendly smile. "Hi. I'm Louisa Dustin and this is my little brother, Barrett."

Barrett eyed Joey up and down, taking particular interest in that world-class shiner. "Hey. I know you. You're a second grader, too, aren't you? You have Ms. Sheen, right? I'm in Mrs. Billings's class."

"Yeah," Joey mumbled. He looked uncomfortable around the other children, but she figured after a few minutes of Barrett's chatter, he would unwind.

"I had Ms. Sheen two years ago," Louisa said. "She's super nice."

Joey didn't look as if he particularly agreed and Hope had to wonder if teachers weren't quite as nice to troublemaking boys as they were to sweet, well-behaved girls.

Hope fought a sudden urge to straighten the boy's wool beanie and tighten his scarf. Something about this unhappy little boy made her want to hug him close and promise everything would be all right, even though she knew it likely wouldn't—not when his mother was heading for prison.

"So what's the plan here?" Rafe asked. "Do you want me to start on the repairs at the lodge?"

"Actually, I had another idea in mind, if you don't mind. These boxes are the lights that go on the Christmas village. I figured while the weather is somewhat nice, we can hang them all and then test the elves to make sure they work."

"Oh, yay! That's my very favorite part!" Barrett exclaimed.

Louisa suddenly looked sad. "We always helped our dad and Uncle Claude do it."

Hope gave her a quick, sympathetic hug. "I know, honey. I'm sorry."

Louisa let out a sigh but quickly turned her attention to other things, in the way of children. "Can I help lead the reindeer?"

"I was hoping you would, darling."

"Wouldn't it be easier to use a pickup truck?" Rafe asked.

She made a face. "Easier, yes. But this isn't about easy. It's tradition to have the reindeer help with this part."

He looked doubtful but followed along holding Joey's hand after Louisa ordered Twinkle and Sparkle to "Walk on" then led the reindeer pulling the dozen or so boxes of lights about three hundred yards to the area surrounded by a picket fence that contained eight small structures they lovingly called the Christmas village.

Uncle Claude had made each little cottage and the animatronic figures inside. It was one of her favorite parts of The Christmas Ranch—from several buildings containing little wooden elves who actually appeared to be hammering and sawing toys to one containing a family opening presents to Mrs. Claus's kitchen, where the animatronic Mrs. Clause perpetually removed cookies out of the oven for Santa.

The village even had a little church—steeple, Nativity scene and all—as well as two little animatronic church mice who raced back and forth.

"Cute," Rafe said as he took in the scene.

"It *is* cute. It's adorable. Kids go crazy for the village, especially at night when all the scenes are turned on and the figures are moving around. It's Christmas magic at its very best."

She was almost daring him to disagree. Something told her Rafe hadn't had enough Christmas magic in his life.

To her delight, he only nodded. "I can imagine. Where do we start?"

"The lights are pretty self-explanatory. Uncle Claude and Travis were both great at organization, which makes it easy on us. Each building has a couple boxes of lights that go to it. They are all clearly marked and there should be a picture of the finished product in each so you know how to hang the lights. You and the boys take a couple of buildings and Louisa and I will take a couple. We should be able to finish in a few hours."

He looked doubtful at that estimate and she couldn't blame him. Every job she had started on The Christmas Ranch was taking longer than she expected, which didn't exactly bode well for the opening—but they had to start somewhere and the Ranch's beginnings seemed the perfect place.

Chapter Seven

He could think of worse ways to spend a November afternoon.

The air was clean and pure, scented with pine and sage and something earthy that wasn't at all unpleasant. Raw mountains towered over the ranch on both sides—it was in a canyon, after all—yet even with their snowy crowns they seemed warm and comforting, rather than forbidding.

As the sun went down, the shadows lengthened, stretching out across the landscape in fanciful shapes. The temperature was chilly but not freezing. He heard the cry of a hawk soaring on the current and the distant whinny of a horse—or maybe it was a reindeer. What did he know. Did reindeer whinny? He had no idea.

He wasn't a country boy. Never had been. He grew

up in the gritty streets of urban Los Angeles, with concrete and gangs and graffiti.

But there was a peace here he had found in very few other places.

Joey seemed to have picked up on it, too. He had lost his shyness somewhere during that walk out here with the reindeer and now he and Hope's nephew, Barrett, were chattering away like best friends.

He strung another line of lights around the window of the little village church while he listened to them talk about their favorite Star Wars character and how the Clone Wars cartoon series was better than the original series. He strongly disagreed but decided to keep out of the discussion for now.

After a moment, the conversation drifted to what they wanted for Christmas.

"I want a new snowboard," Barrett said. "After Christmas, we can ride the tow rope up the sledding hill anytime we want and snowboard down. It's so fun. You should come try it. If I get a new board, you can use my old one."

"I won't be here after Christmas," Joey said, with a dark look at Rafe, who pretended he wasn't paying attention. "We're moving to California right when Christmas vacation starts."

"California? Why would you want to go *there*?"

"Because he's going to get a job there or something, I guess. I don't know. It sucks."

Barrett digested this for a moment, then glanced at Rafe and said in what he probably thought was a low voice but which carried clearly in the cool air, "How come you live with your uncle? Where's your mom and dad?"

Joey frowned. "I don't know where my dad is. He's a *pendejo.*"

Rafe winced and hoped Barrett didn't repeat the word to his aunt, who was sure to know it was a particularly nasty pejorative.

"I don't know what that word means," the other boy admitted.

"It means he's a dumbass," Joey said, which wasn't a much better word. Out of the corner of his gaze, Rafe saw his nephew give him a careful look to see if he was paying attention. When he continued to focus on hanging the lights, the boy continued, "He ran off when I was born."

"What about your mom?"

"She's in trouble and has to go away for a while, so I have to live with my uncle."

"That *does* suck," Barrett said. After a moment, he offered a confidence of his own. "My dad died this summer."

"Did he get shot?" Joey asked, which just about broke Rafe's heart that his nephew had any exposure to a world that would lead him to jump immediately to something so violent.

"No. He died in an accident. I miss him a lot. So now I just live with my mom, my aunt Celeste, my great-aunt Mary and now my aunt Hope, I guess, since she came back."

"All girls?"

Barrett nodded. "I know! I'm the only boy, except for Jack Frost. That's my dog."

"Dogs don't count."

"Jack does because he's super smart, the smartest dog in the whole wide world. He can commando crawl across the room and he can wash his face with his paws and he even kicks a soccer ball."

"No way!"

"Seriously. Maybe if you come back tomorrow, I can bring him and show you."

The two boys went on to discuss the brilliance of Jack Frost, who apparently wasn't even white, despite his name—go figure!—but was a very light-colored yellow lab. They were still at it, stopping only when he would ask them to hand him something up on the ladder.

He was almost finished when a new voice intruded into the nonstop conversation.

"How's it going, guys? It looks fantastic from here."

He looked down from his position on the ladder to find Hope standing just below him. The fading sun picked out the golden highlights in her hair and she looked as fresh and beautiful as the mountain landscape around them.

"We're good. Almost done with this one," he answered.

"That's good. I was thinking we should probably stop for the night. It's after six and it's going to be dark in a minute. If I don't get Louisa and Barrett back to the house before dinner, Faith will be after my head for keeping them out this late."

"I just want to finish this structure. I'm close."

She nodded and turned to Louisa. "Why don't you and Barrett take Sparkle and Twinkle back to the pen and unhitch them?"

"Really? Can I?"

"Sure. You've had plenty of experience. I know your dad let you take care of them all the time."

The girl beamed, thrilled at being given the responsibility.

"Can I help?" Joey asked.

"You'll have to ask your uncle that."

Joey gave him a pleading look out of big brown eyes, the same expression Rafe always had a tough time resisting. "Please, Uncle Rafe?"

He glanced at the reindeer with those big, scary-looking antlers.

"You're sure it's safe?" he asked Hope again.

"Very safe. They're as gentle as a lamb. More gentle, actually. I've known some pretty aggressive sheep in my day."

It was only a few hundred yards to the reindeer pen. From the ladder, he should be able to see them go the whole way.

"I guess it's okay, then."

"Can we ride on the wagon?" Barrett begged.

"Sure," Hope said, "as long as you sit still and don't move around to shift the weight."

Joey and her nephew climbed onto the back of the wagon and held on as Louisa took the lead line on Sparkle and ordered the reindeer to walk on.

His nephew was riding on a wagon pulled by reindeer, led by a girl only a few years older than he was. He supposed that wasn't too strange. In Afghanistan, he had seen girls not much older than Louisa who lived with their family goats by themselves in the mountains for weeks at a time.

"They're fine," she assured him. "Let's finish this so you can get out of here."

"Right."

He turned back to the last string of lights he had to hang and continued attaching them to the little light holders along the lines and angles of the building.

The whole time he worked, he was aware of her— the pure blue of her eyes, her skin, dusted with pink from the cold, the soft curves as she reached over her head to hand him the end of the light string.

"That should do it for me," he said after a moment. In more ways than one.

"Good work. Should we plug them in so we can see how they look?"

"Sure."

She went inside the little structure at the entrance to the village, where she must have flipped a few switches. They had only finished about half of it but the cottages with lights indeed looked magical against the pearly twilight spreading across the land-scape as the sun set.

"Ahhh. Beautiful," she exclaimed. "I never get tired of that."

"Truly lovely," he agreed, though he was looking at her and not the cottages.

She smiled at him. "I'm sorry you gave up your whole afternoon to help me but the truth is, I would have been sunk without you. Thank you."

"You're welcome. I can finish these up when I get here in the morning, after I take Joey to school. Now that I've sort of figured out what I'm doing, I should be able to get these lights hung in no time and start work on the repairs at the lodge by midmorning."

She smiled at him again, a bright, vibrant smile

that made his heart pound as if he had just raced up to the top of those mountains up there and back.

"You are the best Christmas present ever, Rafe. Seriously."

He raised an eyebrow. "Am I?"

He didn't mean the words to sound like an innuendo but he was almost certain that sudden flush on her cheeks had nothing to do with the cool November air.

"You know what I mean."

He did. She was talking about his help around the ranch. He was taken by surprise by a sudden fierce longing that her words meant something completely different.

"I'm not sure I've ever been anyone's favorite Christmas gift before," he murmured.

She gave him a sidelong look. "Then it's about time, isn't it?"

As soon as she said the words, she quickly changed the subject. "Louisa is probably just about done taking care of the reindeer. I should head over to make sure she doesn't need help."

"What about the other lights? Where do you want them?"

She glanced at the few remaining boxes he and the boys had unloaded from the wagon that hadn't been hung yet. "Let's just store them in the front cottage so they'll be ready for tomorrow."

Between the two of them, it only took a moment for them to carry the boxes to the cottage and then Hope turned off the lights and they walked side by side back to the reindeer pen.

"Barrett said something about how fun it would

be to have you home for Christmas, for once. You're apparently one of his favorite aunts."

She chuckled. "I hope I at least make the top three, since that's all he has, if we count Aunt Mary."

"Why haven't you been home for Christmas, since you obviously love it so much? What were you running from?"

It was a question he hadn't intended to ask and one that she obviously wasn't expecting. She stared at him, bristling a little. "Why would you automatically assume I was running from something? Maybe I was running *to* something. Or maybe I just like running."

"Is that it?"

"My sisters and I grew up traveling around the world. Our parents were medical missionaries. My dad was trained as a physician's assistant and my mom was a nurse and they opened medical clinics slash outreach centers all over the world. We never spent longer than six months anywhere. Liberia, El Salvador, Papua New Guinea, Cambodia. You name it, we probably lived there. Until I was thirteen, I probably spoke other languages more than I ever had the chance to speak English. I guess it was just natural for me to inherit the travel itch from them."

He didn't need to ask what had happened when she was thirteen. Again, he had the impression that now was the time to tell her he had participated in the rescue but he ignored it. He was enjoying this tentative friendship they were developing and the heady attraction simmering between them too much to ruin it yet.

"You're home now," he pointed out. "Does that mean you've scratched the itch sufficiently, then?"

She was quiet as they walked through the field, their boots crunching on dry growth. "I don't know. I'm supposed to start another teaching job after the new year but I'm beginning to think perhaps I need to stay here and help Faith and Celeste and Aunt Mary. Things are kind of a mess around here."

"Will you be able to stick around in one place?"

"That is an excellent question, sailor." She gazed up at the mountains around them. "J.R.R. Tolkein said something about how not all who wander are lost. I agree with that. I also believe sometimes a person can be perfectly content wandering around for a long time and then...she's not. I think it was time for me to come home. Past time, probably."

"I hope it's everything you want."

She smiled at him and he had the thought that he could get used to this, too. Walking with a lovely woman across stubble fields as the sun dropped behind the mountains and the stars began to peep out. "Thanks. What about you? What are you going to do now that you've left the navy?"

He was much more comfortable *asking* the deep questions than answering them. "I don't know that either. We're sort of in the same boat. I've got a buddy in private security back in San Diego. He's offered me a job but I haven't decided yet. Who knows? I might want to try my hand at construction. I guess we're both at a crossroads with our lives, aren't we?"

She looked struck by that observation. "It's scary as hell, isn't it?"

He laughed gruffly. "Terrifying," he admitted. "At least you're not responsible for a troubled kid."

"There is that," she said with a smile.

He suddenly wanted rather desperately to stop right there in the field and kiss her senseless, even though they were just a few dozen yards from the reindeer pen where he knew the children waited. He was drawn to her in ways he didn't quite understand. His entire adult life, he had kept his relationships casual and uncomplicated. He had never been this fiercely, wildly attracted to a woman.

He couldn't be completely certain but he suspected she was feeling the heat spark and seethe between them, too. She blushed when he looked at her and he had caught her gaze more than once on his mouth, as if she were wondering what he tasted like.

He let out a breath. This was *not* the time to put that to the test, as tempted as he might be. And he was *very* tempted.

He was glad he resisted when Barrett and Joey hurried over to greet them just seconds later.

"*There* you are," Joey exclaimed. "What took you so long? Guess what, Uncle Rafe! I got to help take the harness off Sparkle and he's not scary at all. He licked my face and it tickled. I fed him a treat *and* I got to pet a dog named Tank and Barrett has his own horse named Stinky Pete and he said maybe I could ride him sometime and I'm going to borrow his old snowboard when it snows more and guess what? You don't even have to walk back up the hill 'cause you just hold on to a rope and it tows you back up and it's fun as can be. Can we come back when it snows more?"

Rafe struggled a moment to make the shift from sheer, raw lust to trying to make sense of a seven-year-old boy's rapid-fire chatter.

"Whoa. Slow down, kid."

"Can we come back tomorrow? Maybe I can ride Stinky Pete then."

"We're coming back tomorrow," he said.

"Yay!"

"But you have work to do, remember? You're paying back Ms. Nichols for breaking her window. We won't be here to play."

His face fell. "Oh, yeah."

"Tell you what," Hope said with a warm smile to Joey. "If you work really hard to help us tomorrow and Friday—and if you and your uncle aren't too busy on the weekend—you can come back and ride Stinky Pete then. Deal?"

"Yes. That would be great. Thanks. Thanks a lot!"

He blinked a little, taken by surprise at Joey's excitement. Who would have guessed that some reindeer and a floundering Christmas attraction would be the things to hit the right button with his nephew and help him feel a little joy again?

He never would have expected it but he wasn't about to look a gift horse—or reindeer—in the mouth.

Chapter Eight

Hope had a million plates spinning and all she wanted to do was find a warm corner where she could curl up and take a nap.

She yawned for about the hundredth time and checked her watch. It was barely 9:00 a.m. and she had already been up for hours—with no naps on the horizon in the foreseeable future.

Mustering all her strength, she shoved the small post hole digger deeper into the hard ground, then set the stake in, tamped the dirt around it hard and moved on to the next spot. Three down, only about a thousand more to go.

Each walking path to the Christmas village, the sledding hill and the main house was usually bordered by waist-high strings of white lights, hung on stakes spaced at regular intervals—and each year, the stakes needed to be reset into the ground.

She drew in a breath and let it out in a huff of condensation then shoved down the post hole digger, thinking how much easier this would have been on a warm day in September than now, when the ground was almost frozen.

"What are you doing and why don't you let me do it for you?"

She had been so focused on the job, she hadn't heard Rafe arrive. He stood beside her wearing a flannel work shirt over a dark green henley. Her knees suddenly felt wobbly but she told herself that was simply because she had only slept a few hours.

"Oh. Hi! Sorry. I didn't hear you come up."

"You looked a little busy."

She made a face. "It's a stupid job. I don't know why Uncle Claude or Travis didn't install these posts permanently so we wouldn't have to reposition them each year. I guess they wanted flexible walking paths in case they wanted to change things up, but it makes tons more work. I thought about skipping it this year but it really does help people know where to go and keeps the crowds contained a little."

"Give."

He was obviously a man used to giving orders. Must be a military thing. The woman-power part of her instinctively wanted to bristle at his highhandedness—but on the other hand, woman power was all well and good but not when it came with a side of stupid. She was tired, her shoulders were already aching after only three posts and he had all those lovely muscles to help with the job.

She handed over the post hole digger with alacrity. "You don't have to order me twice, sir."

He smiled at her pert tone. "Looks like you're spacing them about six feet apart."

"Yes, just so the light strings will drape nicely. It goes faster as a two-person job. If you dig, I'll set the posts."

"Sounds like a plan."

For the next several moments they worked in a companionable silence, settling into a comfortable rhythm. It was hard work but his help took a formidable task and made it much more manageable.

"Thanks for coming," she said. "I wasn't sure if you would really show up or not."

"I told you I would. Did you doubt I meant what I said?"

She had a feeling he was definitely a man of his word. "No. I just thought you might have come to your senses in the night and realized we were fighting a losing battle here." The list of things she needed to do kept growing larger by the minute and she was beginning to fear the disheartening reality, that her sisters were right and she could never whip The Christmas Ranch into shape in only a week and a day.

"I've been in my share of battles. If you want, I can give you all kinds of cheesy idioms about sticking to your guns and so forth."

"Please don't."

He chuckled. "Okay. But how about this one— sometimes you just have to buckle up, put your head down and plow through whatever comes until you get through?"

"I'll take that one," she said. Her sudden yawn on the tail end of the word came out of nowhere and took her completely by surprise. "Sorry."

"Rough night?" he asked, with a mix of amusement and concern in his expression.

"Too short, anyway."

She probably looked like death warmed over. She suddenly had a completely vain wish that she had bothered with a little concealer that morning for what she was sure were probably king-size circles under her eyes. Or any makeup whatsoever, for that matter.

"I can sleep in January, right? I need to strike while the iron's hot and all that. Is that a battle idiom?"

He shoved the post hole digger into the next position, twisted it and with what seemed like hardly any exertion managed to do in about three seconds what had taken her a good five minutes. "I think that one falls more in the blacksmith category. Either way, that doesn't mean you should wear yourself to the bone over this place. How late were you working out here?"

"I didn't do anything else down here on the Ranch. I was up at the house. I'm working on a little side project."

"Because you obviously need a few more of those."

She made a face at his dry tone while she stuck the next stake in the ground in the hole he had dug. "This project is more for fun than anything else. My sister wrote this great story about Sparkle the reindeer and how he uses cleverness and a little magic to save Christmas at the North Pole. I decided to illustrate it and have some copies printed up to sell at the gift shop."

"Of course you did."

"I've got this friend who was in the Peace Corps with me. Now she and her partner own a printing company in the Seattle area and she's agreed to rush print a couple hundred of them for me. If I can get the illustrations to her special delivery by Saturday, there's a chance they'll be here next week but definitely the week after the opening."

"Like you didn't have enough to do?"

"I know. But the story is wonderful and I wanted to share it with the world. I think it will be a huge hit—and the illustrations I've come up with are actually really cute, if I do say so myself. Some of my best work. I've been working on it at every opportunity. I finished the cover last night. I've got a couple more pages to finish tonight before I send it off to Deb and Carlo in the morning."

"Another all-nighter, then?"

"I slept a few hours. Not enough, but a few. Anyway, it will be worth it. It's adorable. Wait until you see the book. The title is *Sparkle and the Magic Snowball*. Isn't that perfect?"

She pushed a strand of hair out of her eyes and smiled at him.

"Perfect," he agreed.

"I'll give Joey a copy before you leave, so he can remember his time working for the crazy Christmas lady."

He shook his head and headed for the next spot. "I don't think he'll need a picture book to remind him of his time here, but I'm sure he'll appreciate it. He couldn't talk about anything else last night at dinner. He can't wait for the chance to ride Stinky Pete."

"He seems like a great kid—now that he's sworn

off throwing snowballs at cars and breaking windows, anyway. Barrett was bubbling over all night at dinner about his new friend. They really seemed to hit it off."

"It's good to see him making friends. The kid has had a tough road. My sister hasn't exactly been the most stable of mothers, moving him around the country from boyfriend to boyfriend, dead-end job to dead-end job."

She had a feeling he needed to talk to someone and she was more than willing to provide a listening ear, especially since she found everything about him fascinating.

"Is that what brought her to Pine Gulch? A man?"

He grunted and shoved the post hole digger into the ground with more force than strictly necessary. "Yeah. A jackass by the name of Big Mike Lawrence. He runs a tavern in town. The Lone Wolf."

Her grimace was involuntary. The place always gave her the creeps. It was decent enough, the time or two she went there with friends during visits home, but she always had a weird feeling there. In comparison, The Bandito—Pine Gulch's dingy, preferred drinking establishment—seemed almost warm and inviting.

Rafe didn't miss her expression. "Yeah. That's the sense of the place I get, too. She met him through an online dating service and after only a few weeks of chatting, he talked her into quitting her waitress job in California and coming out here to work for him."

"I'm guessing it wasn't a wise decision."

"You could say that. He turned out to be selling illegal prescription drugs out of the back room and embroiled her in the whole thing—using and selling. Four months later, she was arrested after a DEA undercover investigation. She agreed to plead guilty in exchange for her testimony but she's still going to serve time. She should have walked away when she showed up in Pine Gulch and discovered her new romance wasn't all he pretended to be online."

He loved his sister. She could hear it weaving through the frustration. "Sounds like she got in over her head."

"I guess. He didn't pull her into the drug operation until she had been here a month, though I have a feeling he got her using right away. It wouldn't be the first time. By then, she claimed she used all her savings to get established here and didn't have anywhere else to go. I don't know why she didn't just call me. I would have helped her. I would have come in and busted any heads necessary and gotten her the hell out of here."

Hope didn't know his sister at all but from her short acquaintance with Rafe, she already knew he wasn't the kind of man a woman wanted to disappoint. His sister probably knew Rafe would come in swinging and might end up hurt.

"She called you to help with Joey, didn't she?"

"I guess."

They had reached the entrance to the Christmas village. He crossed the path to head back to the entrance and shoved the post hole digger into the ground at the next spot with more force than absolutely necessary. She was grateful she had given him a physical task—or he had taken it over, anyway—to work off some of that frustration.

"What kills me most is that Cami knew better. *Knows* better. We lived it, you know? Our mom threw her life away on drugs and alcohol. When she wasn't stoned, she was sleeping off her last binge or out looking to score her next one. We were in and out of foster care or couch surfing with relatives through our whole childhood."

"Oh, Rafe. I'm so sorry." She thought of her own childhood. It might have been ramshackle and even dangerous in some people's eyes, but until her parents died, her family life had always been filled with laughter, with fun, with love. Her parents had always cared passionately about their family, their faith and the people they served.

She couldn't imagine what sort of uncertainty and pain he must have known, in contrast.

He looked embarrassed, as if he regretted saying anything. "I can't understand how Cami could live through what we did, knowing the toll it took on us firsthand, yet still be out there making some of the same mistakes."

She tried to picture him as a little boy Joey's age, trapped in dark circumstances beyond his control while he tried to be protective of his sister. Many young men would have taken the easier route, into that world of drugs and crime and despair. Instead, he had joined the navy and become someone good and honorable, a man who would give up his career to take care of his family.

"My dad used to tell us that everybody has demons," she said softly. "You can't judge a person by the path they've traveled, only the direction they're heading now."

"What would your dad say about the two of us, who don't quite know what direction we're heading right now?"

She smiled a little. Her father would have liked Rafe. She suddenly knew it without a doubt. "He probably would have said we'll figure things out in our own way, that perhaps we're only waiting to find the right door and that when we do, we'll know just which one we need to open."

She shrugged. "But then, some would say he should have left a few doors closed in his life or picked a different one."

"Why would they say that?" His voice sounded interested but his gaze was focused on the post hole digger.

She pictured her father the last time she saw him, quite obviously dead on that jungle path while soldiers shoved her and her sisters into the helicopter. Hope fell silent as she waged an internal debate about whether to tell him.

It wasn't as if she lived her entire life around the events of that Christmas day but they had certainly served as a pivotal moment of her life. It had shaped everything that came after, had really shaped the woman she had become, and she suddenly wanted him to know.

He had shared dark, difficult aspects of his life with her and she had a sudden, inexplicable need to do the same—though it was something she rarely discussed, even with close friends.

"When I was a girl, we lived in a remote area of Colombia for a few months while my parents opened a medical clinic there—until one day my family was kidnapped by leftist rebels, hoping to score a large ransom. The only problem was, my parents really weren't associated with any big umbrella organization. There was no one to pay the ransom. We were held for three weeks, until we were eventually rescued by the US military. My dad died during the rescue and my mom died two months later of a fast-moving cancer that could have been prevented if we had lived in a place with halfway decent medical care instead of out in the middle of nowhere without even a satellite phone to call for help."

He had paused digging to focus on her as she spoke and listened with an unreadable expression. Tension seemed to vibrate off him like the fragile wisps of condensation coming off the warmer dirt they overturned.

"I'm sorry, Hope. So sorry."

Her gaze flashed to his at the low, intense note in his voice. He was genuinely upset by what she said, she realized. Instantly, she regretted saying anything. She shouldn't have brought it up—she probably *wouldn't* have, if she hadn't been exhausted.

"No. I'm sorry. That sounded bitter, didn't it? I'm not bitter. My parents genuinely wanted to help people. My mother used to quote Mother Teresa all the time, that a life not lived for others is not a life. My parents lived their convictions, which is both rare and admirable in this world."

"That doesn't comfort a lost thirteen-year-old girl, does it?"

She narrowed her gaze. "How did you know I was thirteen?"

He turned back to his work and made another

hole. "I don't know. I think the other day you mentioned coming here when you were that age. I guess I did the math."

"Well, you're right. I was thirteen. Fae was fifteen and CeCe was eleven. We were lucky. Relatively speaking, I guess. After our dad died and our mom was diagnosed and put on hospice, we came here to live with Mary and Claude."

Despite the difficulty of the memories, she still had to smile. "Let me tell you, that was some serious culture shock. We went from living all over the world and speaking a dozen languages and dialects to a cattle ranch in small-town Idaho."

"Did you have a tough time fitting in?"

She shrugged. "You can't grow up the way we did without developing some chameleon-like tendencies. We did okay. Celeste and Faith thrived with a little more structure and permanence. I guess I was the odd one out, who wanted to see what was over the next mountain range."

"And what did you find?"

She told him a little about the places she had lived, about some of the amazingly courageous women she had met in Morocco and the earnest, hardworking people she had been privileged to know while in the Peace Corps in Thailand. Before she knew it, they had once more worked their way back to the main parking lot.

"Looks like that's it," Rafe said.

She looked around. "Wow. I was so busy talking your leg off, I didn't realize how close we were to the end."

"You sure you don't need me to dig another hole while I'm in the groove?"

"No. Which I'm sure is a relief to your poor arms. Thank you! I can't tell you how much time you saved. See what a few muscles can get you."

"I always figured they'd come in handy some day."

She smiled. Not only was she fiercely drawn to Rafe on a physical level but she was discovering she genuinely liked him. He was a good listener, he seemed to respect her opinion and he had rare flashes of wry humor that seemed to come out of nowhere.

"You are proving to be invaluable, sailor. Who would have guessed the day your nephew threw a snowball through my window would turn out to be such a lucky break for me?"

He gazed at her for a long moment and then cleared his throat. "Where does this go?"

"We store it in the equipment shed. I'll show you."

She led the way to the small shed and opened the door. The place was small, dim and smelled like motor oil. "We usually store it there by the snow-blower."

He carried the post hole digger in and set it in the corner. When he turned back around, she realized how very little room there was inside the shed. They stood only a few inches apart and she was suddenly fiercely aware of him, the strength of him and the overwhelming *maleness*. Instinctively, she took a step back and stumbled against a small workbench.

"Whoa." He reached out to catch her before she could fall and somehow in the process of trying to correct her balance, she ended up caught in his arms—whether by accident or design, she couldn't tell. Not that she was able to give it much rational thought when this was exactly where she wanted to be.

"Careful," he murmured, which seemed to be a particularly appropriate warning.

"Sorry. I'm sorry."

She gazed at him, trying not to think about how warm he was, how comforting that strong chest felt against her.

His hazel eyes glowed from a shaft of light glowing inside the dim storage shed from the open door. Like a jungle cat, she thought. Her blood began to pulse, thick and sweet, and her insides began to buzz with awareness, with hunger, with anticipation.

He didn't seem in any hurry to let her go. They stood inside the doorway of the storage shed wrapped together for several seconds—or maybe minutes or hours. She couldn't be sure. Finally his gaze dipped to her mouth and he murmured something she didn't quite catch—a curse or a prayer, she wasn't sure which—and then he pulled her closer and lowered his mouth to hers.

He tasted delicious and his mouth was warm and determined. She caught her breath. After the first burst of heady shock—wow, the man could *kiss*— her arms slipped around his neck and she gave herself up to the moment and threw her whole heart and soul into returning the kiss.

Chapter Nine

Who knew the doorway to heaven could be found inside a dingy little storage shed behind the St. Nicholas Lodge?

The moment Hope returned his unwise kiss, heat and hunger crashed over like a thirty-foot swell. She was soft, curvy, warm—and tasted heady and sweet, like some sort of thick, forbidden cinnamon and almond pastry he wanted to gobble up in one bite.

On some deep level, he knew this was a mistake but he couldn't seem to help himself. As they had worked together the past hour, he had been desperately aware of her, the lithe curves and the sun-warmed skin and her sweet little mouth that hadn't stopped moving. She was lush and lovely and he was having a very hard time resisting her.

It didn't help that there had been something

vaguely sexual in pounding the post hole digger into the ground time after time—the sweat, the rhythm, the physical exertion. He finally had to force himself to stop watching her bend over to place each stake into the ground.

Yeah, he had been without a woman for a long time if he could get worked up over digging a bunch of holes in half-frozen Idaho soil.

Was it any wonder he hadn't been able to help himself from taking advantage of the moment when she stumbled into his arms? What normal red-blooded—not to mention already half-aroused male—could possibly resist?

Only a kiss, he thought. Just enough to ease both his hunger and his curiosity. He might have been content with that—though probably not, he acknowledged—until she started kissing him back, sweet and sultry and eager.

All thought flew out of his head and he yanked her against him and just devoured her.

The kiss was hot, wild—his hands under her jacket, hers tangled in his hair. A flat surface. That was all he needed. The analytical part of his brain that helped him survive difficult missions was already scanning the storage shed for something that might work even while the rest of him was busy enjoying the kiss. A cot, a table, anything.

The work bench she had stumbled against might have to do, though its narrowness wouldn't be comfortable for either of them...

He was just about to lower her to it, comfort be damned, when a sudden cold gust of wind rattled the door of the shed. She shivered in his arms and he felt as if that wind had sucked the air right out of him.

What was he doing? This was crazy.

He stepped away, his breathing ragged. She still had her eyes closed, her face lifted to his, and it took every ounce of strength he had not to reach for her again.

She was a dangerous woman.

For several days—since he met her, really—he had been trying to convince himself of all the reasons he couldn't allow himself to give in to this attraction seething through him. One kiss and all that careful reasoning headed for the hills.

This wild, urgent need, the edgy hunger, was completely out of his experience. In truth, it scared the hell out of him. He liked being in control of every situation and right now he felt about as in control as a churning leaf caught in a whirlpool.

He drew in a deep breath and then another, fighting for calm. This was stupid. If she knew who he was, what he had done, she would be bashing him over the head with that post hole digger instead of looking at him with those soft, dazed eyes that made him want to yank her against him and kiss her all over again.

For a long moment, the only sound in the shed was their ragged breathing and then she let out a surprised-sounding laugh.

"Well. You certainly know how to take the winter chill off the morning."

How did she do that? He had half expected her to yell at him for distracting her with a kiss. Instead, she laughed and tried to diffuse the tension—making *him* want to laugh, too, even when his thoughts were in a tumult.

He decided to respond in the same casual vein. "Just doing my humanitarian duty. I wouldn't want your lips to freeze off."

She smiled a little. "Thanks. I appreciate that. I'm pretty fond of my lips."

He was growing quite fond of them himself. "They are certainly memorable."

She laughed again, a soft bell of a sound that seemed to slip beneath his jacket and lodge somewhere in the vicinity of his heart.

"Um. Thanks, I guess."

"Right." He paused. "Despite how memorable I find them, I will do my best to forget. Kissing you was...inappropriate. I've been trying to talk myself out of doing it for days but apparently I don't have the ironclad self-control I always thought I did—at least when it comes to you."

"You've really been trying to talk yourself out of kissing me for *days*?"

"Something like that." It seemed like eons—vast, endless eternities. He sighed. "I'm sorry."

"You have nothing to apologize about. We don't need to make a big deal about this, Rafe. You're a great-looking guy—all that sexy warrior mojo you've got going on—and I'm obviously attracted to you. But I'm not in the market for a casual relationship right now. Neither are you. We both have stuff going on. I get that. This was a mutual, uh, lip-warming. Now that we are sufficiently heated, we can get back to business. For me, that business is the thousand and sixteen things I have to do today, not fretting about a moment of craziness that isn't going to happen again."

He should be relieved that they were both on the same page. Instead, he wanted to toss the whole book in the air, push her farther into that little shed and kiss her until they created their own tropical microclimate.

He nodded, forcing down the urge. "Good. That's good. I guess I'll get going on some of the things I wrote down yesterday."

"You still want to help?"

"Of course. Why wouldn't I?"

"I... Great. Thank you. I need to take care of some things in the office. You can find me inside the lodge if you need me."

If he needed her. That was a laugh. He needed her like he needed water and air—but he was going to have to accept he couldn't have her. "Got it. I'll see you later."

She waved and hurried away, leaving him aching and aroused.

Hope hurried inside the St. Nicholas Lodge, pausing only when she was certain she was quite concealed from view.

Inside, she sagged against the wall, fighting the urge to bury her face in her hands.

What in the world just happened there?

That kiss.

She drew in a shuddering breath, grateful for the steady support from the wall. Her knees still felt shaky and she was afraid if she stepped away she would teeter. She tried to tell herself it was merely exhaustion from only catching a few hours of sleep but she knew it was a lie.

Oh, she was in big trouble here.

She pressed a finger to her lips—her apparently *memorable* lips—and closed her eyes, still tasting him there, like coffee and mint and all things delicious.

For several long moments there in the supply shed, she had forgotten everything she had to do. All she wanted to do was stay there. In the circle of his arms, she had been aware of a strange but powerful feeling of security, of safety, as if he would protect her from everything ugly and dark in the world.

Yeah. Big, big trouble.

It was only a kiss, she tried to remind herself. But why did she feel as if something monumental had just shifted in her world?

She could fall hard for a man like him. How could she resist the combination of quiet strength, inherent decency and raw gorgeousness?

As if she needed one more thing to worry about right now! She didn't have *time* for a broken heart, darn it.

For one crazy moment, she wanted to march out there and tell him that while she appreciated what he had done so far, she didn't need his help and he could now just go on his merry way finding some other *memorable* lips to warm, thanks very much.

He would know as well as she did that was a lie, that she was nothing short of desperate. If she wanted to open the day after Thanksgiving, she needed every bit of help she could eke out—even from a man she sensed might have the potential to leave her battered and broken.

She needed Rafe's help. Pure and simple. That had been reinforced to her quite emphatically that morning when his muscles and strength had turned a seemingly impossible job into a big checked-off item on her to-do list.

Where on earth would she find someone else on short notice to take care of everything that needed to be done—and how could she possibly find the time to start the search?

Rafe was here, he was more than capable and for reasons she didn't understand, he wanted to help her.

She would simply have to do her best to forget about that kiss—which just might be harder than the task she had set out for herself to bring Christmas to Cold Creek Canyon.

She wasn't sure how much longer she could keep going at this frenetic pace.

Tuesday night—five days after that stunning kiss, which, of course, she hadn't been able to forget whatsoever—Hope let herself into the darkened ranch house at ten minutes to midnight. Her family was probably sound asleep. Oh, how she envied them. She was so tired, her left eye had started to twitch hours ago, but she still had at least a few hours of work to do before she could give *both* eyes a rest.

For the umpteenth time, she wondered if she was crazy to have ever started this whole thing with The Christmas Ranch. The odds still seemed stacked sky-high against her. With each passing hour, she grew more and more certain she simply wouldn't have time to accomplish everything necessary to open to the public.

Maybe she would have been better off throwing all the time and energy she had expended the past week into the cattle side of the Star N. At least then she would feel like she was actually helping Faith and the rest of her family, not entangling them all in this ridiculous holiday attraction that would probably be a huge bust this year.

She had one more full day and evening to accomplish everything on her list. The day after that was Thanksgiving and she had vowed she would take off at least part of the day to be with her family.

She wouldn't have even come close to being ready for the opening if not for Rafe Santiago.

He showed up as soon as Joey went to school and left only long enough to pick his nephew up and then the two of them would come back and help out until after dark. He was a relentlessly hard worker and didn't stop going from the moment he showed up until he left.

She had no idea how she would ever repay him.

Hope was painfully aware that since that kiss, both of them made a conscious effort to avoid being alone together. Awareness still seemed to shimmer between them, bright and dazzling, but he had been careful to focus on jobs on the other side of the Ranch from wherever she was working.

When they spoke, it was polite, even friendly, but they exchanged no more of those confidences they had shared that day while digging the holes for the pathway light stakes.

That hadn't stopped her from watching him when

he wasn't looking and remembering those heated moments in his arms.

She pushed away thoughts of Rafe, which had the strangest way of sneaking into her mind when she could least afford the distraction. She still had a few hours of work to finish before she could sleep but she needed a little fuel to keep her engine going.

With any luck, Aunt Mary or her sisters—depending on who had cooked that night—might have left her a plate of whatever the family had for dinner.

After hanging her coat in the mudroom, she headed for the kitchen and was shocked to find a light on and Celeste working at the table with art supplies spread out all around her—googly eyes, colorful feathers and construction paper.

"Wow. You're up late!"

Celeste shrugged. "I had a few things to prep for the Thanksgiving storytime I'm doing at the library tomorrow. We're making paper plate turkeys and I've learned the only way to keep things halfway sane is to throw all the kits together ahead of time."

"Those are darling. The kids are going to love them."

Hope knew Celeste adored her job as the children's librarian at the small city library in Pine Gulch and she was wonderful at it—dedicated and caring and passionate.

"Thanks," Celeste said, then gave her a somewhat sheepish look. "Okay, these handouts are only part of the reason I'm still up. I could have done this in my room, but I was waiting for you. I've been dying of curiosity."

"Oh?" For a crazy moment, she wondered if Celeste was going to ask about the big, gorgeous man who was working at The Christmas Ranch, but both of her sisters were so busy, she wasn't sure they were even aware of Rafe and all his efforts on her behalf.

"You got a FedEx delivery this evening. Two big boxes from Seaberry Publishing."

"What?" she exclaimed, her exhaustion instantly sluicing away. "They're here? Oh! That's fantastic news! The best!"

"What's here?"

"Our book! *Sparkle and the Magic Snowball.* My friend Deb was going to rush the print job but she warned me not to expect anything until next week at the earliest. I'm so happy the first shipment of books will be here for the opening!"

"You said you wanted to print up a few copies," Celeste exclaimed, looking suddenly nervous. "Exactly how many was a few?"

"Um. Five hundred." She winced, waiting for her sister's reaction.

"Five hundred!" As she might have expected, Celeste's jaw sagged and her eyes filled with horror. "What are we going to do with five hundred copies of a book no one wants? How much did that cost you out of pocket?"

More than she wanted to share with her sister. She had used a big chunk of her savings but fully expected to earn it back—when the books completely sold out—and enough to give her sister a nice royalty. "Don't worry about it. I got a good deal from Deb and Carlo."

"Five hundred copies!"

She reached for her sister's hands. "CeCe, it's a

delightful story, full of heart and wisdom and beauty. The best sort of children's story. Deb absolutely adored it. She asked if she could print some extras to give as Christmas gifts to her daughter's friends and reduced our cost accordingly. I hope that's okay."

Celeste swallowed hard. Her eyes looked huge in suddenly pale features. "Oh, Hope. What have you done?"

"We talked about this, remember?"

"You said a few copies!"

"It's always cheaper per item if you print more quantity at the same time. That just makes good business sense."

"But what are you going to do with all those books?"

"We don't have to sell them all this year. We can keep them in the gift shop for years to come."

"If we even have The Christmas Ranch after this year!"

She wasn't going to think about that yet. Not tonight, when she finally had something wonderful to celebrate.

"You will love it, I swear. I can't wait to see the finished product. I can't believe you didn't already open the boxes!"

Celeste looked pale, her eyes huge in her narrow face. "They were addressed to you. I couldn't snoop through your personal mail."

Hope certainly would have snooped, but then she and Celeste were two completely different people. Her sister was sweet and gentle and kind and Hope was...not.

She squeezed Celeste's hands. "I'm so glad you

stayed up until I came home. It's only right that we look at them for the first time together. The author and the illustrator. How cool is that?"

Celeste was all but wringing her hands as Hope lifted one of the boxes onto the table and grabbed some scissors out of the kitchen catch-all drawer to carefully split the packing tape.

She pulled the flaps back and her heart gave an excited little kick at the delicious new-book smell that escaped.

There it was, in bright, brilliant colors. She reached inside and pulled one out. Had she really drawn that darling, whimsical picture on the cover, of a reindeer with a wreath around his neck and his little bird friend Snowdrop perched in his antlers?

It seemed only right that she handed the first copy over to Celeste, who took it with hands that trembled. "Oh. Oh, my," her sister breathed, gazing at the picture book as if it contained all the secrets to the universe.

Celeste ran a finger over the little reindeer and for the first time, Hope felt a qualm or two or ten, hoping she had done the right thing.

"It's such a charming story," she said softly. "I'm afraid my illustrations haven't quite done your words justice."

"No. No, they're perfect. You hit exactly the right note between sweet and warm, without being corny."

She flipped through the pages, stopping on one or two to look more closely. "This is crazy. These are fantastic, Hope! When could you possibly have had time to do this? You've only been here a little more than a week!"

"Oh, here and there. A lot of it was at night after everyone was in bed."

This was the reason she was so tired, because she had spent three nights straight without sleep, trying to get all the details right on the twenty illustrations.

"They're wonderful. I love Snowdrop. He's my favorite. Oh, and the way you've put that darling little holly wreath in all the pictures."

She flipped another page with a soft smile. "You're very good," she said. The note of surprise in her sister's voice probably wouldn't have bothered Hope so much if it didn't serve to emphasize the distance that had crept up between her and her sisters the past few years, mostly by her own doing.

"Tell me this," Celeste said. "Why are you off teaching English in far-away countries when you could be a professional illustrator?"

She harrumphed. "You don't need to exaggerate. I'm not *that* good."

"I know books, Hope—especially children's books. It's what I do. These illustrations are fantastic—whimsical and charming and full of wonder and heart. People are going to love it. How could they not?"

"I hope so. I have five hundred copies to sell." At least one of her harebrained ideas just might pan out, though it was too early to know until visitors to the gift shop were able to get their hands on the book. "You'll be receiving fifty percent of the profits, by the way."

Celeste shook her head. "Just put it back into the Ranch. Buy a few more strings of lights or something."

She hoped the book would result in far more sales than that but she didn't say anything now to her sister. It was hard enough for Celeste to know she had printed five hundred copies so she decided not to mention that Deb and Carlo were prepared to go back to press at any moment once they gauged the demand.

"We make a pretty good team, don't we?"

"I guess we do." Celeste smiled, looking soft and lovely. Her sister's beauty was the sort most people tended to overlook. She had always been quiet and perhaps a little introverted—more so after their parents died and the sisters moved here to Pine Gulch.

Perhaps having a published book would give Celeste a little more confidence in herself and all she had to offer the world.

"We should do another Sparkle story together," she said impulsively. "Not this year, of course—I won't have time before Christmas, but will you let me take a look at some of your stories after the holidays? Because of the time crunch this time, I couldn't really consult with you about the illustrations but I'd love more collaboration, if we do another one. I also want you to consider the possibility of creating a digital version to sell online, if we get enough interest with the print version."

Celeste blinked, looking stunned and a little overwhelmed. Hope took pity on her.

"Not tonight. We can talk about it another time, when we're both not so tired and you're not up to your eyeballs in turkeys."

Celeste nodded, her gaze still on the book in her hand.

"And speaking of story times," Hope went on,

"you must take a few copies to the library for the children of Pine Gulch. Three or four, at least. And don't you think it would be perfect if Mrs. Claus—perhaps a professionally trained storytelling version of Mrs. Claus—could come and read *Sparkle and the Magic Snowball* to the children who visit The Christmas Ranch while the real Sparkle is there, too?"

Her sister pushed a strand of overlong hair from her face. "You don't give up, do you?"

"Not when it's about something and someone I care about so much. I would love you to do this. I know I can find someone else to be the official Christmas Ranch storyteller—even Aunt Mary— but no one would be as good at it as you, especially since you wrote the story yourself."

Celeste gazed down at the book in her hands then back at Hope. "I don't know. I'm not sure I can read my own writing aloud. It's such an intimate, personal thing."

"All the more reason you should be the one sharing it with the world. It's your choice. Just think about it. I won't push you, other than to say that I don't think anybody else can really do the story justice, CeCe."

With a sigh, her sister folded her arms, tucking the book against her chest. "You're impossibly stubborn, just like Dad was. I suppose that's one of the reasons we all love you."

"If I weren't stubborn, I never would have taken on The Christmas Ranch. I would have let that Closed Indefinitely sign stay up, well, *indefinitely*, and would have spent the past week getting in everyone's way here at the house and fretting about my next job."

Instead of burning the candle at both ends *and* in the middle—not to mention nurturing a serious crush over a man she couldn't have, but she didn't mention that to Celeste.

After a long silence, Celeste spoke, her words hurried as if she had been thinking them for a while and only needed the chance to let them out.

"This is hard for me to admit, but...but I think what you're doing with the Ranch is a good thing. The *right* thing. For all of us."

"Oh. Oh, CeCe." Her throat suddenly felt tight and her eyes burned, though she told herself it was only the unexpected approval from her sister.

"The children have been happier these past few days, with something to keep them occupied. Even Faith has remarked on it, though she might not admit it out loud to you. Mary is happier too and even Faith seems to have more energy. We were all completely frozen in our grief over Travis. Maybe we just needed you to come shake things up. I'm glad you're here and I'm glad the Ranch is going to open after all."

"Does that mean you'll help out as Mrs. Claus?" she pressed.

Celeste rolled her eyes. "You don't give up, do you? I'll think about it. That's the best I can do right now. And now I really need to catch some sleep if I'm going to be able to cope with thirty preschoolers tomorrow."

"Good night. I'll be right behind you. I'm going to grab a bowl of cereal and read this beautiful story written by my brilliant baby sister one more time."

The brilliant baby sister in question only gave a

rueful smile and, clutching the book, headed for her room, leaving Hope behind to wonder whether she was really doing the right thing for her family.

Chapter Ten

The next afternoon, Hope made the finishing brush strokes on the project in front of her, then sat back on her heels to admire her work.

Beautiful. Exactly the look she wanted. She had found the big piece of scrap barnwood from an old demolished outbuilding behind a shed on the Star N and that weathered red was exactly the shade she wanted.

Okay, it hadn't been a top priority, but she didn't mind the extra time she had spent on it, especially with her sudden conviction that the sign would provide the perfect finishing touch.

Maybe CeCe was right. Maybe she should have tried to be an illustrator. She had always loved to draw and paint and had a fair talent at it. She had a degree in art history but had always thought she didn't have the chops to do it professionally.

The last few years while in Morocco, she had turned to photography, not only because the country was so very photogenic but because it seemed a far more portable medium—it was easier carrying a camera and lenses through a crowded, twisting medina than a huge canvas and box of paints.

Photography was definitely an art form but she did love the immediate, hands-on, almost *magical* connection between her brain, her eyes, a canvas and the brush in her hand.

She stood up, pressing a hand to the small of her back that ached from an hour crouched over the floor in the back storeroom of the St. Nicholas Lodge.

"What's all this?"

She turned at the voice and found Rafe had come in while she was patting herself on the back over her work. He looked gorgeous, dark and tough and ruggedly handsome in another of those heavy cotton work shirts over a soft henley, this one blue.

Her palms suddenly felt itchy and her insides trembled. "New sign for the reindeer enclosure," she managed.

"Home of the Original Sparkle," he read aloud.

She was particularly proud of the cute reindeer on the sign and the way the word *Sparkle* seemed to come alive.

"Remember I was telling you about the delightful story my sister wrote and the illustrations I was doing for it?"

"Right. The reason you haven't been getting any sleep since you came back to Pine Gulch," he said.

"Well, the books came last evening and they're

absolutely wonderful, every bit as magical as I dreamed."

"Sparkle is one of the reindeer you had pull the wagon that day we put the lights on the Christmas village, right?"

"Yes. We all adore him. He's gentle and kind and definitely a favorite. I've got to show you something. You get to be the first one to see it."

Overflowing with excitement, she hurried over to her big tote bag in the corner. She reached inside and pulled out the little project she had made up after mailing off the finished pages of the book to Deb and Carlo in Seattle—a stuffed fabric reindeer based on her illustration, made out of sparkly fabric, complete with a ribbon and child-safe jingle bell around his neck.

"Ta da. It's Sparkle."

She thrust it at him. The toy looked a little girlish and silly in his big, rough hands as he turned it this way and that for a better look. "You did this?"

"I like to sew. All of us do. It's something our mother taught us."

"You sew, you paint, you teach English in undeveloped areas of the world. Is there anything you *don't* do?"

Besides protect her heart against big, gorgeous navy men? She was discovering she wasn't all that terrific at that particular skill.

"Don't you think the kids will love it?" she asked, ignoring his question.

He gave her a look filled with amusement and something else—something warm and bright and even more glittery than the little stuffed fabric creature he held in his hand. "They will adore it. I just have one question."

"What's that?"

"Do you ever stop moving?"

She shrugged, though she had been living in a state of perpetual exhaustion for days. "I'll stop after the opening Friday."

"No, you won't. You're going to work yourself into the ground until Christmas is over. You can't do everything you want to, Hope. If you don't pace yourself and figure out the definition of the word *enough* you're going to find yourself flat on your back in bed."

She would like to be flat on her back in bed—as long as he was there beside her, cuddled in front of a fire, with a nice cozy quilt wrapped around them and nothing else.

The impulse came out of nowhere, probably a product of her exhaustion. Suddenly she tingled *everywhere*. Stupid imagination.

"I know. I don't need a lecture from you, Dr. Santiago."

He made a face. "You need to listen to someone. You need to slow down, Hope. You're wearing yourself out. I'm...worried about you."

"Oh."

Warmth fluttered through her, sweet and seductive.

"You don't need to worry about me. I'll be fine. Great. Only two more days and then the Ranch will open and everything will be perfect."

"And you'll be in a hospital bed, suffering from exhaustion. What do you have to do this afternoon?

Just give me your list and I'll do what I can to check things off while you go take a nap."

"I wish that were possible, but it's not. I have too much to do if I'm going to make this happen."

"Let me help you, Hope."

"You are helping me! You've been amazing, Rafe. Anything I need, you're there, from fixing the tow rope to building that little shelter where people wait in line for the sleigh rides to all the repairs you've done inside and out. I honestly don't know what I would have done without you. Are you sure you don't want to come work full-time for me on The Christmas Ranch?" she joked.

"Depends," he said, his voice husky. "What kind of benefits can you offer?"

All at once, she knew he wasn't talking about 401(k)s or long-term disability insurance. The air between them was suddenly charged, thick and heady, swirling with the currents of awareness they had both been ignoring all week.

Walk on, she told herself, just as if she were one of the reindeer pulling a sleigh. *You're hanging by a thread here anyway and don't need his kind of trouble.*

Apparently she wasn't very good at listening to her own better judgment. She took a step forward, unable to help herself.

"I'm sure I could come up with something... enticing."

His laugh sounded rough and a little strained. "I don't doubt that."

She wanted to kiss him again. All week, the memory had simmered beneath her skin. They had both worked so hard. Surely they deserved a little reward...

She stepped closer and he suddenly looked wary, as if he regretted ever starting this.

"Um, Hope."

She kept moving, until she was only a foot away from him. "I've been telling myself all week that kissing you again wouldn't be a very good idea."

He cleared his throat. "Yeah. I get that."

"Right now, I don't care. I'm going to do it anyway. Is that a problem for you, sailor?"

He laughed again, his pupils a little dilated. "Ask me that again in a few minutes," he said, his voice a low rasp that shivered down her spine. He didn't wait for her to kiss him, but reached out and tugged her against him and lowered his mouth.

Oh. Wow.

Their kiss in the little storage shed had been raw and wild. This one was soft, sweet, tender—and completely devastating.

He explored her mouth with his, each corner, each hollow, licking and tasting and seducing with every passing second. She was fiercely grateful for his muscles and his strength. Without him holding her up, she would have collapsed right onto her cute little reindeer sign.

"You taste so good," he murmured. "I've dreamed about it every single night since that morning last week. I thought I imagined it but you're even more delicious than I remembered."

She didn't care about anything right now, not the Ranch, not the storybook, not her to-do list. All that mattered was this moment, this man and the amazing wonder of being in his arms again.

She wrapped her arms around him, savoring the heat and strength of him. A warm tenderness seemed to unfurl somewhere deep inside, something she had never known before that made her want to hold him close and take away all his worries. She didn't want it to ever end.

He slid his mouth away and began to trail kisses across her cheekbone to her throat and then worked his way back to her mouth.

Yeah. She would have no problem standing right here and doing this for the rest of the day. Or week. Or year.

"Oh."

The soft exclamation—and the realization that someone else was there—finally pierced the soft, delicious haze that seemed to have surrounded them. It took her a moment to collect her scattered thoughts enough to be able to ease her mouth away from his.

She turned and found Faith standing in the doorway, watching the two of them with her mouth open and an expression of raw shock on her features.

Rafe had suddenly gone still, like an alert, dangerous panther, she realized, though she wasn't quite sure why. Maybe the same reason why she suddenly felt mortified, though she was a grown woman who had every right to kiss an incredibly hot—and even more amazingly *sweet*—man if she wanted to. And she *so* wanted to.

"Faith. Um. Hi."

Her sister continued to stare at them, though her gaze was fixed on Rafe.

"Um, Faith, this is Rafael Santiago. The man I told you about, who has been helping me out with the Ranch."

"You never mentioned his name."

Why did that matter? Hope shrugged. "Didn't I? That's funny. I'm sure I must have."

"No. Believe me, I would have remembered."

After the sweet intensity of that kiss, Hope could barely focus on remembering to breathe, forget about trying to figure out why her sister was behaving so oddly—and Rafe, as well, for that matter. Why would he be watching Faith with that strange, alert expression?

She was suddenly reminded forcefully that he had just spent twenty years in the military, facing dangerous situations.

"What are you doing here?" Faith demanded, in a weird, almost hostile tone that was totally unlike her usually gentle sister.

"Faith," she exclaimed, mortified. "I would think that was fairly obvious." *And if you would please go away, we can do it some more.*

"Not *that*," Faith said. "I'm asking what *he* is doing here?"

"Helping out your sister," Rafe answered for himself.

"Why?"

"Because she needed it. And because I wanted to."

Faith stepped forward and Hope was surprised to see some of the color had leached away from her features.

"Why are you in Pine Gulch, of all places?" she

pressed. "That seems an odd coincidence, don't you think?"

"That's exactly what it was, actually. Believe it or not." A muscle worked in his jaw as he turned to look at Hope with an expression she couldn't read, almost like an apology, though she had no idea what was happening here.

"It's also a long and complicated story."

"Is it?"

"My sister is in jail in Pine Gulch. I'm here caring for her son until after her sentencing."

"And you just happened to bump into Hope and offer to help her with The Christmas Ranch?" Faith asked, skepticism in her voice.

"That's about the size of it, yeah."

Okay, this was ridiculous. She knew her sister felt a great deal of responsibility for her and for Celeste but this was pushing things. She was thirty years old, for heaven's sake, and had spent most of her adult life not only living on her own but residing in a completely different country.

"Faith, cut it out. Why are you being like this? Rafe has been an amazing help to me. I never would have been ready for the opening Friday if not for him."

Her sister narrowed her gaze at Hope, looked at Rafe, then back at her with an intensity that suddenly made her uncomfortable. "You don't know who he is! You don't remember him at all, do you?"

Hope frowned. "Remember him? What are you talking about?"

"Special Warfare Operator Rafe Santiago. He was

there, in Colombia. One of the navy SEALs who came to our rescue."

Her heart gave a hard, vicious kick at the words and for a moment, she could only stare. "That's ridiculous," she said, when she could find her voice again.

"It's not," Faith insisted. "I remember every single name, every man. I wrote them all down so I wouldn't forget afterward."

"You sent thank-you notes, care of our lieutenant," he said, his voice gruff.

Through her shock and disbelief, she saw Faith's too-pale skin suddenly turn blotchy and pink as she blushed. "It seemed the right thing to do."

She shifted back to Rafe, suddenly flashing back to that horrible Christmas day, to stunning hazel eyes in a tense, hard face.

She remembered gunfire and shouting in Spanish and the helicopter and then screaming and screaming for her father while a young soldier yanked her inside.

"That was...you?"

Rafe had grown even more still in that eerie way he had, that jungle cat, as if he were fusing himself into the background, merging his skin and his bones to his surroundings.

"Yes."

"You said you were in the navy. You never said you were a SEAL."

He said nothing. Where was the man who had kissed her so tenderly? Who had held her and whispered delicious words about her mouth and how she tasted?

This man seemed like a stranger—dark, dangerous, indestructible.

"You've known all this time and you never said a word about being there. We even *talked* about Colombia and you still didn't mention anything. Why?"

"It was...wrong not to say anything, especially when you brought it up. I should have. I'm sorry now that I didn't. I tried a few times but the moment never seemed quite right."

This was the reason he had helped her, she suddenly realized. Not because they were friends, not because he was coming to care about her as she was him. It was all tangled up in the past, in that pivotal moment that had altered the course of her life. The fear and the pain and the helplessness she couldn't outrun, no matter how far she traveled.

She stared at him, feeling as if everything had changed in a matter of moments, as if all the soft, hazy daydreams she was beginning to spin about him had just turned into the dark, ugly stuff of nightmares.

Chapter Eleven

Okay, he had seriously mucked this whole thing up.

Rafe did his best not to stagger beneath the combined weight of the glares delivered by the two Nichols sisters.

He thought he had been doing a good thing, helping the family out by making The Christmas Ranch ready for guests, but somehow he had made several serious errors in judgment.

He should have told her. In retrospect, he wasn't sure why the words had been so difficult. At first, he hadn't wanted to dredge up something he knew must be difficult for her or add another layer of stress when she was already dealing with so much.

Later, after he had come to know her better and—yes, he could admit it—to *care* about her, he had put off telling her because he had been trying to avoid this moment, the shock and betrayal in her eyes.

He supposed some part of him had also worried that when she found out he had been involved in her family's rescue, she would tell him to stop coming to The Christmas Ranch. That would have broken Joey's heart, since his nephew loved coming here every afternoon—and without his help, she never would have been able to whip the place into shape in time.

In the back of his mind, he had known she would find out eventually. It was as inevitable as deep snow in the mountains around here.

"You knew who I was from the beginning," she said with dawning realization. "That very first day, when Joey threw a snowball at my pickup truck."

"Not until you told me your name," he said. "After that, yes. I knew you and your sisters had come to Pine Gulch after everything went south in Colombia. Our lieutenant made a point of keeping track of your whereabouts and passed that intel along to those of us he knew were concerned about you all."

"You've probably been on hundreds of missions since Colombia," Faith said. "How could you possibly remember three girls you met seventeen years ago?"

"I remember everything about that day." He didn't tell them it was his first mission as a SEAL and his first actual combat experience and it would have been indelibly etched in his brain even if everything hadn't fallen apart as it had. "When Cami called me and told me she was in jail in a little town she was sure I'd never heard of called Pine Gulch, Idaho, I was stunned at the way fate could twist and turn like a python."

He should have told her, damn it. That very first

day, he should have mentioned they shared a history. Each and every time the thought had come to him over the past week that *now* would be a good time, he should have acted instead of sitting on his ass and waiting for the perfect moment.

He might have told himself he was thinking about her feelings but the truth was, withholding the information hadn't been fair to her.

"Before that day with Joey and the window, I always intended to come out here and meet all three of you. In the back of my head, I guess I thought maybe I would check and see how you were, all these years later. I couldn't quite figure out how to just show up on your doorstep and say, 'Hey, surprise. Remember me?' I guess I just never expected to meet one of you on the other end of a broken car window."

The explanation didn't appear to ease any of the stormy emotions he could see building in Hope's expression. She faced him, all tangled blond curls and kiss-swollen lips and flushed cheeks.

"You've been working here a week and you didn't think it was important to bring it up once. You *kissed* me—multiple times, I might add—and you still never told me."

Faith cleared her throat. "I should, uh… I've got some things to do at the house."

Right. Just come on in and interrupt in the middle of an epic kiss, ruin everything, then leave again.

He knew the thought wasn't fair. He was the only one to blame in this whole mess.

"You don't have to leave," he and Hope both said at the same time.

"I think I do. I only stopped to see how things

were going down here and…to see if you need a hand with any last-minute things."

"Oh, Faith." Something he didn't understand passed between the sisters, something intense and emotional. Hope crossed to her sister and hugged the other woman, though he wasn't quite sure why.

"Thank you. I can't tell you how much that means."

Faith hugged her back for just a moment then extricated herself. "I'll come back after I, um, finish some things at the house."

She clearly wanted to escape. Rafe couldn't blame her. He wouldn't mind slipping away either. Before he could, Faith approached him and gave him a steady look. "Has Hope invited you and your—nephew, is it?—for Thanksgiving?"

The question took him unawares and he had to collect his thoughts for a moment before he could answer. "Yes," he admitted.

"I've invited them over a few times," Hope said, with dawning awareness. "He refused each and every time. Now I'm beginning to see why. You couldn't be sure Faith or Celeste wouldn't be as ditzy as I apparently am. You figured one of them would recognize you."

Yeah, that had been part of the reason for his continued refusal, but not the entirety. "I told you I didn't want to intrude on your family dinner."

"It's no intrusion," Faith assured him. "Come to dinner, if you don't already have plans. It's the least we can do to repay you—not only for what happened seventeen years ago but for all the help you've apparently given Hope these past few days."

She waved to both of them and hurried out of the lodge, leaving a heavy silence behind.

"Well," Hope finally said. "This is an unexpected turn of events."

He drew in a breath and faced her. Her usually bright, open expression had become hard, almost brittle, in the past few moments.

"Hope. I'm sorry. I should have told you."

"Why didn't you?"

"Stupid reasons," he admitted. "I see that now. I didn't want to upset you when you were already stressed and exhausted."

He exhaled. He might as well get this over with, tell her the rest of it while every ugly secret was bubbling up like an acidic mineral pool.

"At first, I didn't tell you because, well, I didn't know how to bring it up. Later, I suppose it was... self-protective, in a way."

"What are you talking about?"

"I made mistakes in that raid. Mistakes that have haunted me ever since. They're hard to admit, especially now that I've come to know you and better understand the cost of my mistakes. It was my first mission and I screwed it up. That's why I never forgot any of you, why I was interested in your well-being after the mission was over. That's also why I didn't want to tell you after we became...friends. I guess I didn't want you to hate me."

She stared at him, eyes huge in her delicate, lovely features. "What mistakes? How did you screw up?"

"We don't need to go into this now, do we?"

"What mistakes, Rafe?" she pressed, her tone relentless. He knew that stubbornness. The same grit had kept her on the go constantly the last week, until she was about to drop from little sleep. She wouldn't let up until he told her everything, each ugly misstep.

"We can at least sit down."

Not knowing quite what else to do, he gestured toward the chairs arranged around the huge Christmas tree she and the children had decorated a few evenings earlier, near one of the massive river rock fireplaces.

He sat down next to her and fought the urge to reach for her hand. This was much harder than he expected. He had spent seventeen years as a freaking navy SEAL and had scuba dived, parachuted and prowled into all manner of hazardous situations. So why was his adrenaline pumping harder than he ever remembered?

"First of all, I guess I should tell you, this was my very first operation as a SEAL. I was a dumb twenty-one-year-old kid just weeks out of BUD/S. I spent my first few years in the navy stationed on an aircraft carrier and had never been in actual combat."

She was silent, watching him out of eyes that didn't seem to miss anything.

He swallowed. "It was supposed to be an easy extraction, just sneak in during the early morning hours when everyone was sleeping, separate you and your family from Juan Pablo and his crazy militants and take you all back to the helipad. But something went wrong."

"Yes. It did."

He closed his eyes, reliving the confusion of that night. "Your father was my responsibility but he wasn't being held where he was supposed to be, where our intel reported."

"They moved him to another hut a few days before Christmas to keep him separate from our mother and us, thinking he wouldn't try to escape without us and we couldn't escape without him."

"My partner and I finally found him. He was being guarded by one small kid who looked like he was no more than thirteen or fourteen."

His sister's age, he remembered thinking. "I should have taken him out in his sleep but I...didn't."

He should have at least immobilized the kid and removed any threat with a sleeper hold, but the kid had already been sound asleep, snoring like an elephant and he and his partner had made the disastrous decision to leave him sleeping.

"We managed to get your father out of his restraints and the hut where they were holding him. But just as we were heading to the extraction site, something awoke his guard—the kid I didn't have the stones to take out in his sleep. He yelled and all hell broke loose as you all were loading up. I turned to fire but I was too slow."

"And?"

He swallowed. "If I had been a fraction of a second faster, your father might still be alive."

He waited for her to get angry or hurt or *something*. She only continued to stare at him out of those huge eyes.

"You said the mission haunted you for all these years," she finally said. "Is this the pack full of guilt you've been carrying?"

"Not all of it, but it makes up a few of the heaviest stones I've got back there."

"Well, you can set those down right here. What happened to my father wasn't your fault. He made his own choices, all along the way. He was the one who chose to drag his family to that particular area, despite all the warnings. My father was a great man whose heart was always in the right place but he was also an idealistic one. He believed in the inherent goodness of people and he refused to accept that some people and some situations couldn't be fixed by an outpouring of love or charity or generosity of spirit."

"My single moment of hesitation cost your father his life."

She shook her head. "You don't know that. A helicopter was landing outside Juan Pablo's camp. Do you really think that guard or Juan Pablo or anyone else would have slept through that? You risked your life for us. All of you did. That's the only part that matters to me about your actions of that day."

She genuinely meant it, he realized. He had expected tears and recriminations, anger, pain. Instead, she was offering *solace*.

What an amazing woman.

Her words seemed to seep into his heart, his conscience, like a balm, healing places he hadn't realized were damaged, and he didn't trust himself to speak for a long moment.

"I'm not angry with you about anything you did that day. I couldn't be."

Her voice abruptly hardened. "Don't think for a moment that lets you off the hook for keeping this from me since the day we met. You owed me the truth from the very first."

"I did," he said, his voice gruff. How could he tell her he hadn't wanted to risk damaging this fragile, tender friendship that was becoming so very important to him?

"I don't know if I can get over that, Rafe. It's going to take some time." She stood up. "That said, Faith is right. You and Joey should come to Thanksgiving dinner. You have no excuse to say no now. We eat about three. I'll tell Mary and Celeste to expect you."

She rose, gave him a long look, then hurried away from him into the office of the lodge and closed the door.

By the time she made it to the office, Hope was almost running, though she hoped Rafe couldn't see her from where he still sat by the fireplace.

With a pretend casualness she was far from feeling, she closed the door with great care so it didn't slam then sank down into Uncle Claude's big leather chair, desperately needing the comfort of the familiar.

She had barely had time to absorb the sweetness and aching tenderness of that kiss and *this*.

She didn't have time to even think straight right now. In forty-eight hours, The Christmas Ranch would be opening to the public and she still had a hundred last-minute details to attend to—not to mention more reindeer to sew, if she could find time.

She had promised herself she would take Thanksgiving afternoon off to be with her family, which left her tonight, a few hours in the morning and Friday throughout the day, before The Christmas Ranch had its traditional opening at dusk on the day after Thanksgiving.

Now she had this stunning revelation to contend with.

Rafe was there. He was a navy SEAL and had been involved in her family's rescue that fateful Christmas day seventeen years go.

Now she realized why he had seemed so familiar. She had blocked many things out about that day but now that she knew the truth, memories flooded back in a heavy deluge.

She couldn't have pinpointed any particular features among any of the other SEAL team members who had rescued them except those eyes, so unexpectedly and strikingly hazel in his otherwise Latino features.

Now she could picture him as clearly as if she had a photograph of that day—young, tough, dangerous.

Why hadn't he told her?

She still didn't understand. She thought they had been able to push aside their obvious attraction for each other and had started to develop a friendship of sorts.

She had even begun to think maybe she was falling in love, for the first time in her life, even though she had known nothing would ever come of it.

How could it?

For one thing, he obviously didn't share those burgeoning feelings if he could continue perpetuating a lie by omission. More important, he was completely focused on his nephew right now, as he should be. In a few weeks' time, he would be moving back to

San Diego to start a new life with Joey and she had all but decided she was going to stay here in Pine Gulch with her family.

For another, how could she ever trust him now?

She buried her face in her hands for only a moment, surrendering only briefly to the pain and frustration churning through her. She had worked so hard to move past that life-changing day, to tell herself she was stronger than what had happened to her. She wouldn't let the ideas of some misguided zealots control her life.

Now, when she had finally met a man she thought she could fall in love with, the events of that day reared back to consume everything good and wonderful in her world.

After a momentary pity party, she dropped her hands, rubbed them briskly down her legs and stood up again. She didn't have time for this. The people of southern Idaho didn't care about her petty problems. They needed a little Christmas spirit and she was going to deliver it, damn it, no matter what the cost.

Chapter Twelve

They shouldn't have come.

Standing beside him on the front porch at the Star N Ranch house, Joey vibrated with excitement. It was like a force field of crackling energy around him.

"Can I ring the doorbell?" he asked.

"Sure. Go ahead."

The boy rang it, waited about two seconds, then rang it again. He was about to go back for a third time two seconds after that but Rafe held a hand out to block him.

"Whoa. That's good. Give somebody time to answer the door."

"I'm starving. I can't wait for turkey!"

Before Rafe could answer, the door opened and a vision appeared, silhouetted in the doorway. It was Hope, but as he'd never seen her before. She was wearing makeup for the first time he remembered and all that luscious hair had been curled. It fell past her shoulders in blond waves that made him want to trail his fingers through it.

She wore dressy slacks and a soft-looking sweater in rich blues and greens.

His mouth watered—and not because of the delicious aromas emanating from the warm doorway.

"You came," she said, her features politely distant. "I wasn't sure you would."

"You basically ordered me to," he answered.

She made a face before returning her features to that cool mask he couldn't read. Was she happy to see them? He didn't know. She seemed to have walled up some central part of herself since that earthshaking kiss the day before and the awkward way it had ended, with her sister's interruption.

"Hey, Joey." She beamed down at his nephew with a much more genuine smile that made his chest suddenly ache.

Yeah. They shouldn't have come.

"Hi, Hope. Uncle Rafe said we should bring you a hostess gift, so I made this." He thrust the handprint turkey he had made that morning.

"I love it! Thanks. That one is going on the fridge, for sure. Come in. You don't have to stand out in the cold."

They walked into the house. He had caught delicious smells while standing on the porch, but once inside, Rafe was just about bowled over with sensory overload from multiple delicious things cooking. Potatoes and turkey and stuffing and pie, all mixed together in one luscious package.

Through it all, he could still pick up Hope's scent, though; that subtly exotic cinnamon and almond scent of her.

"Where's Barrett?" Joey asked as soon as he handed over his coat.

"He and his sister are down the hall with a few of the neighbor kids, engaged in a vicious Mario Kart competition in the den. I believe there's always room for one more. Third door on the right."

"Yay! Thanks!" He hurried away from them, leaving Rafe and Hope alone in the foyer.

"You brought goodies," she said, gesturing to the casserole dish he held.

"Er. Yeah. I believe we've already firmly established I'm not much of a cook but I've been known to make a pretty good guac from one of my grandmother's recipes. I brought chips, too."

"Wow. Thank you. Those will go fast. Everybody's in the kitchen. Come on back."

He followed her toward those delectable scents and found the open kitchen and family room more crowded than he expected. To his relief, he wasn't going to be the only male at the Star N family Thanksgiving. Two other men were in the room.

An older woman, plump and comfortable, looked him up and down from her spot at the long kitchen table where it looked as if she was snapping beans. "So this is your navy SEAL."

"He's not mine," Hope said, her voice tight. "But yes. This is Rafe Santiago. Rafe, this is my aunt Mary and these are a few of our neighbors, Chase Brannon—who has a ranch just up the road—and Justin and Ashley Hartford. Yeah. That Justin Hartford."

He stared for just a moment at the familiar face of the man holding out his hand before he recovered enough to shake it. He didn't get starstruck, but every single one of Hartford's films was in his top ten list of favorite films. He knew the man had left Hollywood more than a decade earlier and disappeared from public view. Now he knew where he'd gone.

"And you know my sisters already."

He nodded warily at the sisters, not sure of what his reception would be now that everyone in the family knew he had been involved in that ill-fated rescue.

The youngest sister—the quiet one who wrote stories about reindeer and worked as a children's librarian, he remembered—rose from the table and approached him. To his great surprise, she reached up and kissed him on the cheek.

He was still reeling from that unexpected sweetness when she pounded him lightly on the chest. "You should have told us."

He squirmed. "Yeah. Hope has already given me the lecture."

"Told you what?" Ashley Hartford, blond and pretty, asked him.

"It's a very long story." Faith stood at the stove stirring something he couldn't see from here while the big, burly rancher handed her ingredients. "Let's just say our family owes him a huge debt that all the Thanksgiving dinners in forever could never repay."

That was so far from the truth they weren't in the same time zone, but this didn't seem the time to argue about it.

"So what brings you to Pine Gulch?" Justin asked. "Are you visiting or are you new in town?"

"Another long story," he said, trying not to think how weird it was to be making small talk with a man whose movies he had watched too many times to count. "Visiting, I guess you'd say. I'm only here until Christmas. I've got a...family situation in the area."

"Well, if you have to be stuck somewhere for a while, Pine Gulch isn't a bad spot," Hartford said with a smile.

"True enough," Rafe answered, surprised to realize he meant the words.

When he first came to town, he had felt a little claustrophopic with the mountains looming big in every direction, as if he didn't quite have enough room to breathe or a ready escape route in case of trouble, as ridiculous as that seemed. With each passing day, he was coming to appreciate the wild beauty of this corner of the country and the inherent kindness of the people.

Now that he was apparently becoming a more familiar face around town, neighbors had started to wave to him when he drove past, parents in the car pool lane at school stopped to chat and one of the checkers at the grocery store had even special ordered a certain kind of protein drink for him, after he couldn't find it the other day.

He would be sorry to leave—something he never would have expected three weeks earlier when he rolled into town.

"Can I do anything to help in here?" he asked.

Faith shook her head. She still hadn't smiled at him and he wondered if she would—not that he was narcissistic about it. The woman had just lost her husband. She had plenty of things on her plate that had nothing to do with his sudden reappearance in their lives.

"I think everything is just about ready," she said in answer to him. "In fact, now that the gravy is done, I think it's safe to call in the kids."

The meal wasn't the awkward experience he might have expected. The food was delicious and beyond plentiful and the company quite convivial. All the children—Faith's and the Hartfords's—were included at the main table. Joey seemed to fit right in and he only had to remind him once, in a subtle, private way, not to talk with his mouth full.

The neighbors were obviously good friends—he got the impression Ashley Hartford was particularly close friends to Faith and Celeste and the big rancher Brannon seemed protective and solicitous of all the Nichols women.

Listening to the conversation, it was obvious Hope and her sisters loved each other and their aunt and all of them doted on Faith's children.

After dinner, everyone helped clean up, even the kids. He had some vague expectation that he and Joey would take off as soon as the dishes were done, as he planned to make a visit to Cami at the jail before visiting hours ended, but his nephew jumped right back into playing video games with the other children in the den and he didn't have the heart to drag him away yet.

The adults moved into the family room, where Chase Brannon had turned on a football game.

"Oh, look," Celeste exclaimed, gazing out the window. "It's starting to snow a little again."

"Keep your fingers crossed it stays that way," Hope said darkly. "The little part, I mean."

"Don't say that!" Justin said with a laugh. "After that dry autumn we had, we need all the precipitation we can find."

"You can have your precipitation, cowboy, as much as you want. The day *after* tomorrow," Hope said.

"A big storm on opening day is bad for business," Faith explained to Rafe, still without smiling at him. "A few inches, like we had overnight, is just perfect but people don't like to brave nasty weather just to watch some little twinkling lights come on."

"One year we had two feet of snow on Thanksgiving night," Mary said.

"Keep your fingers crossed we get a few picturesque inches and that's all," Hope said. "Which reminds me. I've got to run down to the barn."

"You promised you would take the afternoon off," Faith said.

"I know, but I left a mess down there. I was oiling and polishing the reindeer sleigh and checking all the bells and I'm afraid I let the time get away from me. I just need to put all the cleaning supplies away and hang all the harnesses back up. It will only take a minute."

"Can't it wait until tomorrow?" Celeste asked.

"It could, but I don't want to risk one of the barn cats knocking anything over and making a bigger mess. I'll be back in a minute."

She rose and though he knew it was likely a mistake, Rafe rose, as well. She hadn't given him more than that polite smile all afternoon and he wanted to get everything out in the open between them if possible. This might be his only chance to clear the air.

"Need a hand?" he asked.

"No. I'll be fine."

"Don't be silly," her aunt Mary said. "With two people, the job will take half as long. Plus, he can make sure you don't get distracted by a hundred other tasks you find to do once you walk out that door. I'll tell you one thing, missy, we're not waiting on you all night to break into those pies."

He could tell she still wanted to refuse his help and was clearly reluctant to have him come with her. The thought stung, though he knew he deserved it.

After an awkward moment, she shrugged. "Sure. I can always use help with the heavy lifting."

In the foyer, she handed him his coat and he helped her into hers and they walked out into the crisp November night. A light snow was falling and even though he judged it was only about four-thirty in the afternoon, the cloud cover made it seem later and darker.

"Thank you for a wonderful dinner," he said, as they headed down the path toward the St. Nicholas Lodge. "I'm not sure Joey has ever enjoyed himself so much."

"I didn't do much," she admitted, "but I'll be sure to pass along your thanks to Mary and Faith. You said Joey enjoyed himself. What about you?"

"Everyone was...more kind than I expected." Or deserved, he thought, but didn't add. He also didn't mention that by *everyone*, he meant present company excepted, since she wouldn't even look at him.

He didn't like the distance between them but

didn't have the first idea how to bridge it. "What will you need my help with tomorrow?" he finally asked as they neared the reindeer barn. "Joey and I can be out first thing."

"I was going to talk to you about that, actually. I'm glad you brought it up."

"Oh?"

"Joey has worked so hard this week. Throw in the work you did that you won't let me pay you for and we are more than square for the broken window on my truck. I could have replaced it three or four times over for the in-kind work you have done."

This wasn't about the window and it hadn't been since almost the first day.

"I'm just saying, you've done more than enough. You can stop now. You don't have to come out tomorrow and Joey can consider his debt more than paid after all his hard work—not to mention yours."

"We'll be here tomorrow," he said firmly. "If you don't need me after that, okay, I can accept that. But do you really think I'm willing to put all this work into something and not stick around to see the payoff?"

She sighed. "Fine. Thank you. I do still have many things to do before dusk tomorrow and I'm sure we will encounter some crisis or other that will benefit from your carpentry or mechanical skills."

He didn't feel like he had much of either one but he had learned quickly while he had been helping out this week—everything from repairing the motor on a couple of the little animatronic scenes in the Christmas village to figuring out the electrical load capabilities of the wiring inside the lodge and how many strings of Christmas lights it could safely support.

As they neared the barn next to the reindeer enclosure, Hope lifted her face to the cold air, heedless of the snowflakes that landed on her cheeks and tangled in her eyelashes. His chest ached with some indefinable emotion as he watched her. Regret? Longing? He wasn't sure.

"This storm has me nervous," she finally said, taking the last few steps to the barn. "The weather forecasters are saying we're supposed to get several inches. It could be a disaster."

"Or it could put everybody into even more of a holiday mood. You never know."

She opened the door and flipped on a light switch. Most of the reindeer were outside, preferring the cold weather, he supposed, though they could come in and out of the barn through the open door on one side.

The place smelled of leather, oil and hay—a combination he found more appealing than he might have expected.

A small fancy red sleigh that looked like it could only hold two or three people was parked in one concrete stall.

"Wow. I haven't seen this before. That's impressive."

"It's been in the other barn closer to the house. We just brought it down this morning. Uncle Claude loved this. He babied it all year long. It's kind of silly to go to all this work to polish it up, since we only use it a few times during the season for special events."

"Why?"

"The reindeer aren't that crazy about being hitched

up together so we don't do it very often—mostly for photo ops. We park it in front of the lodge some afternoons and hitch one or two of the reindeer to it. Kids love to have their picture taken in it since it looks like they're driving Santa's sleigh."

"I can see that."

They spent a few minutes picking up the cleaning supplies she had left out and storing them in a cabinet in what she called the tack room, then they hung up the leather harnesses adorned with bells that jangled as they hung them up.

"Thanks," she said. "See. I didn't need your help. What did that take? All of five minutes?"

He shrugged. "I would rather be here with you than inside talking to people I don't really know."

Even if everyone inside the house had been lifelong friends, he would still rather be out here with her in the quiet peace of this barn, while snow fluttered down outside and the sun began its slide behind the mountains.

"Are you going to the jail to see your sister today?"

So much for quiet peace. He sighed at the uncomfortable topic. "Yeah. I figured we would stop by after we leave here. The jail is open for special visiting hours on Thanksgiving. I promised her I would bring Joey, even though I don't think it's an environment he needs to spend much time in, you know?"

"I get that."

"This whole thing is such a mess. Frankly, I have no idea how Joey is coping."

"He seems to be doing okay. He's a hard worker and he's obviously a smart kid. He has been nothing but polite to me while he's been working around here for me. Once the two of you get back to San Diego and settle into a routine, he'll be fine. You'll both get through this."

He still wasn't convinced of that. The idea of returning to San Diego held much less appeal than it had a week ago, even though his buddy with the private security firm had called him twice this week, wondering if Rafe could start right after Christmas.

"Thanks. I appreciate the vote of confidence. Every day I feel like I'm discovering another part of raising a kid that hits me completely unprepared."

"You're doing fine, Rafe. Better than fine. Joey seems happy and healthy. He's a very lucky boy to have you."

Her words seemed to seep into his heart and he wanted to keep them there. "Do you mind calling me about twenty times a day to remind me of that?" he joked. "That should just about be enough."

She smiled, the first genuine one she had given him all day. She looked so beautiful there in the rustic old barn, with her wild, pretty hair and the delicate touches of makeup. He felt a little tug in his chest, remembering that earthshaking kiss of the day before.

He knew he had no right to kiss her again but the emotions welling up in his chest basically made it impossible for him to do anything else.

The moment his lips touched hers, everything inside him seemed to sigh with joy. He didn't understand this emotional pull between them. It was unlike anything he had ever experienced, rich and fierce and *real*. Maybe it had something to do with the past they shared or maybe it was simply because of her, this amazing woman who had come to mean so much to him. He didn't know. He only knew that kissing her was the best kind of magic and he never wanted to give it up.

On some deep level, Hope knew she should push him away. How could he kiss her again, as if nothing had changed between them, when *everything* was different now?

This wasn't, she amended. The sweetness and peace she found in his arms was somehow the same, despite everything else between them. How could that be? She wasn't sure, she only knew she wanted to hold on to it as tightly as she could manage.

She had a wild wish that they could stay right here, sheltered together in this warm barn while the snowflakes twirled outside and the wind began to moan a little in the rafters.

Oh, how she wished everything could be different between them, that they had met each other at a different time, a different place and without all the ghosts of the past haunting them.

"Hope," he murmured against her mouth. Just her name, and her heart seemed to tumble in her chest.

She was in love with him.

The realization washed over her with stunning clarity.

She loved Rafe Santiago. Rescuer, navy SEAL, reluctant guardian.

Oh. What was she going to do? Not open herself up for more emotional devastation, that was certain.

"Stop. Rafe. Stop. Please."

He groaned low in his throat and rested his forehead against hers.

This was heartbreak. It was a physical, tangible pain in her chest and she wanted to cry, much to her horror. The tears welled up in her throat, behind her eyes and she had to take a moment to force them all back before she could speak.

"What are we doing here?" she whispered.

He eased away. "If you don't know, then I obviously must be doing something wrong."

She made an impatient gesture. "Here. You and me."

He looked wary suddenly. "What do you mean?"

This was a mistake. She should be casual and light, pretend their kisses meant nothing to her. She didn't need to flay herself open to him.

She couldn't do that. This was too real, too important. She could feel her hands trembling and she folded them together "Every time you kiss me, you turn me inside out. You don't have any idea, do you?"

He stared at her, those beautiful hazel eyes wide in his dark features and a little wary. "I...do?"

She wanted to be angry with him for being so oblivious to his effect on her but she couldn't. How could she blame him, when she was the fool here?

"You probably also don't have the first clue that I could...easily develop feelings for you. I'm halfway there. I could fall hard for you, Rafe. I don't want that and you don't either, trust me. I need your help to make sure it doesn't happen."

It was only a little lie. She wasn't halfway anything, but he didn't need to know that part—especially when he didn't bother to conceal his shock. He swallowed hard, staring at her. "Hope—"

She gave a short laugh. "I know. It's a mess. Believe me, I don't *want* to care about you. This *thing*—

this heat, this attraction, whatever you want to call it—is crazy and intense and completely the last thing I need right now. When you kiss me, I lose track of everything I want, everything I've worked for. All I want is to stay right here in your arms."

He cleared his throat. "Why is that a bad thing, again?"

She ground her teeth, fighting the urge to smack him. He didn't get it. He didn't see she was fighting to earn her family's respect. She owed them. She suddenly remembered another Mother Teresa quote her mother used to say—*Bring love into your own home, for this is where love must start.*

She hadn't done that. She had left her family behind while she went off trying to change the world in some misguided effort to do what little she could to carry on her parents' legacy.

Meanwhile, she hadn't been here for her family when they needed her after Travis died. This was her chance to make things right for them. By making The Christmas Ranch a success, she might be able to help save the Star N—but not while she continued to let him distract her, while she fell apart each time he kissed her.

"If I let you, Rafael Santiago, you will break my heart." She straightened and gave him the most steady look she could muster. "There's only one solution to that. I just won't let you."

"The last thing I want to do is break your heart."

"And the last thing I want to do is fall in love with you and then have to stand by with a broken heart while I watch you walk away."

"What if I don't? Walk away, I mean?"

Despite his careful tone and guarded expression, she felt a tiny flutter of joy, fragile and sweet—which she firmly squashed beneath her boot.

"You would. You have a life in San Diego and you need to return to it. I get that."

"I don't have to go back to California. You said it before. We're both at a crossroads."

"If you didn't—if you stayed—I would always wonder whether you are doing it for the same reason you volunteered to help at the Ranch in the first place. Because of some wrong-headed sense of guilt, to make amends for something you were never responsible for in the first place."

She knew she was being ruthless and even a little cold, using the Colombia card to win her argument, but it was the only way she could protect herself— and she suddenly had the epiphany that she had been protecting herself for a very long time. Maybe even since that fateful Christmas day.

Her relationships were always casual, light, fun... and completely without depth and meaning. She had never had any problem leaving any of the men she dated behind when she went on to the next job, the next adventure.

With Rafe, everything was different. She knew that instinctively. Her heart would break time after time and she couldn't put herself through that.

"Please don't kiss me again. I won't beg but consider this the closest thing to it. If you can possibly feel you owe me anything because of what happened in Colombia, after everything you've done this past week to help around here, *this* is all I would ask. I would prefer if you didn't come around after tomorrow's opening. Will you do that for me?"

She folded her hands together, her nails digging into her palms. She hated asking him. Worse, she hated the hurt in his eyes as she basically told him she didn't want him there anymore. They had begun a friendship before he ever kissed her and she was basically throwing that away, as well.

What other choice did she have?

"I don't know what to say."

"Don't say anything. This is hard enough."

She headed for the door, knowing if she didn't leave now she wouldn't be able to find the strength. "I'm going to head over to the Ranch office in the lodge and finish a few things. Thanks for your help here and with...everything, but you should probably go get Joey from the house so you can visit your sister. I would imagine visiting hours at the jail are limited, aren't they?"

He gave her a long, measured look, his expression murky. She had a feeling he had plenty of things he wanted to say to her but she didn't give him a chance, only turned and walked out of the barn without looking back.

Chapter Thirteen

"Where is everybody?"

Aunt Mary's question was bewildered and completely genuine but it still gouged under Hope's skin like uncoiling barbed wire.

She forced a smile for her aunt and leaned forward to hug her, setting off the little jingle bell on her ridiculous elf hat. "That's a pretty bad snowstorm out there. On a night like tonight, most people want to be home cuddled up by the fire watching *It's a Wonderful Life* or something. They don't want to tramp around in the snow and wind to look at a few lights."

Opening night at The Christmas Ranch usually was one of their biggest events. They offered free hot cocoa and cookies, a live band playing Christmas music and of course the big event itself, when they turned on all the lights in the vast display.

Instead of the two hundred people she had anticipated, she could only see a fraction of that, maybe thirty or so, mostly close neighbors and friends who lived in Cold Creek Canyon.

The Dalton brothers—Wade, Jake and Seth—were there along with their wives. They all stood talking to the Dalton matriarch and her second husband, who happened to be the mayor of Pine Gulch.

Caidy and Ben Caldwell and his children had come, along with Caidy's brother Ridge Bowman and his wife, Sarah, and daughter. The wealthy and powerful Carson McRaven and his wife, Jenna, who had provided the refreshments for the evening, stood talking to the Cavazos—Nate and Emery—as well as Faith's best friend, Ashley Hartford, and her hottie former action movie star husband, Justin, who had just been there for Thanksgiving dinner.

Those who lived in Cold Creek Canyon were always supportive of The Christmas Ranch, which meant the world to Hope and her family.

It wasn't quite enough, though, she thought, looking at the sparse crowd. This was close to a disaster.

"Did you put an ad in the paper, honey?"

She put on a fake smile for her aunt. "Sure did. I called them earlier in the week, but I was too late by then to make the deadline for yesterday's edition. They couldn't run anything until next week's issue since all the Black Friday ads had already been scheduled. Our ad will run in the Pine Gulch community paper as well as the Idaho Falls, Rexburg and Jackson Hole papers next week. A radio spot started yesterday on all the area stations. And I put flyers up on all the community boards I could find in the region."

She was quite certain it hadn't helped their attendance any that for weeks that blasted Closed Indefinitely sign had hung over the gate. She couldn't seem to get the message out—everybody in town still seemed to think they were taking the year off because of Travis's death.

Was she supposed to go door to door throughout town to let everybody know the Nichols family had changed its collective mind—well, okay, she had changed it for them—and the Ranch would now be open for business as usual?

This was no one's fault, she reminded herself. Not Aunt Mary's. Not Faith's or Celeste's. Not really hers either, since she had worked her tail off trying to get ready for tonight. None of them could control the weather or alter newspaper deadlines.

"Things will pick up," she assured her aunt, wishing she believed it herself. "Now, go mingle and have a good time. I'm going to grab another tray of appetizers."

She hurried to the little kitchen off the office and grabbed one of the beautifully prepared trays. At least they had good food. Jenna was an amazing cook, which was why her catering business was enormously successful.

She adjusted her stupid hat a little with one hand then headed back out.

"Can I give you a hand?"

Her heart skipped a little beat at the low voice and at the sight of Rafe, big and strong and gorgeous.

He and Joey had come out earlier in the day to

do a few last-minute adjustments to the tow rope on the sledding hill but she had been busy in the office and hadn't spoken with him. Now, seeing him here dressed up in a button-down shirt and trousers, her breath caught and her knees felt ridiculously weak.

"I like your outfit."

Oh. Son of a *nutcracker*, to steal her favorite epithet from Buddy the Elf. He looked gorgeous and masculine...and she looked like Buddy's dorky little sister.

"I couldn't talk Faith or Celeste into wearing it so I guess I was stuck. Somebody had to."

Though why, she suddenly wasn't sure. No one was even there to see her dressed in the stupid elf costume. "This is a disaster. Only three dozen people—and they're all friends and neighbors."

He looked back through the doorway into the party. "Don't worry. Things will pick up. Word of mouth will spread. As soon as word gets out that you're open this year after all, the crowds will follow."

She didn't deserve his reassuring words, not after the things she had said to him the day before. She couldn't believe he'd even showed up tonight.

All the work the two of them had done ahead of time. For what? A handful of people? She thought of all the money she had poured into this, most of her savings, all the promises she had made to her sisters. This was supposed to be her chance to show them she could contribute to the family.

She gripped the tray harder, fighting the urge to sink down to the floor, appetizers and all, and cry.

"I wish I could believe that."

Rafe gave her a searching look and she knew he must see the emotions swimming in her expression. His hard, formidable features softened. "Yeah, maybe the turnout tonight isn't what you'd hoped, but give yourself a break. It's only the first night."

"I know. I just had such high hopes."

"You've done a good thing here, Hope. You've thrown your heart and your soul into this and people are inevitably going to respond to that. You've brought Christmas magic to Pine Gulch. Everyone needs a little of that right now."

"Even you?"

He looked out at the brightly lit lodge with its big Christmas tree, the blazing fires, the grand Santa throne where Mac Palmer presided in his glorious costume.

"*Especially* me," he said quietly. "I'm honored I had the chance to be part of it."

Her throat felt tight, achy, and she wanted nothing more in that moment than to fall into his arms. How could she possibly resist this man?

He gave her a sudden, unexpected grin that sent heat spiraling through her. "One thing, though. You might want to try to smile a little. Trust me, there's nothing more depressing than a grumpy elf."

She laughed, as he intended, even though her heart seemed to ache. Everything she said the day before had been completely ridiculous, she thought again. She wasn't in any danger of falling in love with him. How could she be, when she was already there?

"Point taken. I will put on my perkiest smile. Thanks for the reminder, sailor."

"Anytime."

Except he wasn't only a sailor. He was a navy SEAL—the toughest, most hardened of warriors— and he wouldn't be here in a few more weeks for pep talks or anything else.

The reminder was as coldly sobering as if someone had just shoved her into a snowbank.

Ignoring the ache in her chest, she pasted on a smile so big it made her cheeks hurt and headed around the crowd with her platter of cookies and hot cocoa.

By the time Monday morning rolled around, Hope was afraid her face had permanently frozen in that rictus of a fake smile.

She pulled the quilt up under her chin, gazing out the window at the pale morning. She could see daylight, which meant it had to be late—on these shortest days of the year, the sun didn't rise above the mountains until almost eight.

She had slept in, the first time in *weeks* she had done that. So why did she still feel achy and exhausted? Maybe because she hadn't dropped into bed until after two in the morning, up late sewing more little reindeer toys so they could at least have twenty or thirty on hand in the gift shop, just in case.

She flopped over onto her back and stared at the ceiling of the odd-angled bedroom that had been hers since she and her sisters came here, lost and afraid.

She was seriously tempted to punch her pillow, pull the covers over her head and go back to sleep for another three or four hours. Why shouldn't she? Why was she putting so much time and energy into what was turning into her most spectacular failure ever?

The crowds had picked up a little on Saturday as the winter storm slowed but on Sunday, attendance had been *way* down.

At this rate, they would barely break even for the season. All her good intentions about helping ease Faith's burden would remain only that. Pipe dreams. Pretty little ice sculptures that melted away into nothing.

She should have just let The Christmas Ranch stay closed and thrown her energy into the cattle side of the Star N operations. She wasn't sure what she could have done there but it would have been better than creating false expectations.

With a sigh, she sat up. As much as she might like to, she had too much to do to stay hidden away up here feeling sorry for herself.

She pushed away, swiveled to the edge of the bed and was just about to stand up when her cell phone rang from its spot charging on the bedside table.

She stared at it for a long moment, recognizing Rafe's number flashing across the screen

She couldn't escape the man. He was in her thoughts, her dreams, and now on her phone. She almost didn't answer it but finally picked it up, unplugged it from the charger and answered.

"Hello." She tried for a brisk, businesslike, *didn't I ask you to leave me alone*? sort of tone.

"Are you watching this?" he demanded, with more excitement in his voice than she had ever heard.

"Watching what?" she asked, not wanting to tell him she was still in bed and wasn't watching anything except a few cobwebs up in the corner.

"The television. Channel six. Are you close to one?"

"Yes." There was a small flatscreen atop the carved old-fashioned bureau, since Faith used this as a guest room when Hope wasn't there. She wasn't sure it worked since she hadn't had time to turn it on once since she had been back in Pine Gulch.

"Hello, Nation. Turn it on, right now!"

"Why?" she asked warily.

"Just trust me. Channel six," he said again. "They were teasing a story right before the commercials I think you're going to want to see."

The floor was freezing against her bare feet as she padded to the television, the phone in the crook of her shoulder. "Not your usual sort of show, is it? Or maybe you like all that celebrity gossip."

"Joey wanted to watch a cartoon this morning before school. I flipped through the channels to find something and happened to catch a couple minutes of this one. It really doesn't matter why I was watching. Just turn it on. Hurry."

She flipped the television on and found the channel. They were just coming back from a commercial to a man and woman sitting together on a set decorated with poinsettias and a Christmas tree.

"Welcome back, Nation. I'm Paloma Rodriguez."

"And I'm Mitchell Sloan. We hope you're having a lovely Monday, wherever you are."

"So, Mitchell. You know my husband likes to ski, right?" Paloma said.

"From what you've said, he likes to ski and you like to sip hot toddies by the fireplace."

"Exactly. I'm not much of a skier. This year we

decided to take the kids to Jackson Hole, Wyoming, for Thanksgiving. It's such a fun little town. We spent a week there and Kent and our older son had a wonderful time skiing. Meanwhile, toward the end of the week, the younger two were starting to drive me crazy—until I happened upon this wonderful little family attraction a short way from Jackson. It was called The Christmas Ranch and look at this."

The woman pulled out a darling little stuffed reindeer—*her* darling little stuffed reindeer!—and Hope shrieked.

"Ow," Rafe said in her ear and she realized she was still holding the phone.

"Sorry! Sorry! That's Sparkle! Are you seeing this?"

"I am."

The camera panned to some home video of two little children bundled up in snowsuits—sledding down the hill behind the Ranch, then cut to them gazing, awestruck, at the reindeer, stars in their eyes.

"This place was so magical," Paloma Rodriguez said with definite gush in her voice. "It's truly wonderful, the most charming place I've seen in a long time. They have live reindeer for the children to pet and even their own little mascot."

She made the stuffed toy do a little dance. "This is Sparkle and he has his own story that is absolutely adorable. Charming and sweet and heartwarming. Alicia and Julio begged me to read it to them at least a dozen times on the airplane ride home and I'm still not tired of it. It's that cute. *Sparkle and the Magic Snowball.* If you're in the area, you should visit. The Christmas Ranch, just outside Pine Gulch, Idaho. It's less than an hour from Jackson Hole and well worth the trip, for the cinnamon hot chocolate alone."

"Great travel tip, Paloma," her cohost said with a practiced smile. "Linda and I are heading to Jackson Hole between Christmas and New Year's. I'll definitely have to try some of that hot chocolate. And speaking of hot. I hear we have some spicy news on the celebrity romance front."

They started chatting about a picture that was apparently exploding all over the internet of a young starlet and her much older leading man in a heated off-screen embrace.

Hope paused the show and flopped back onto her bed.

"Oh. My. Word."

She was still holding the phone to her ear, she realized when she heard Rafe's low chuckle in her ear. It seemed only right that she share it with him since he had worked every bit as hard as she had this past week to get everything ready for the opening.

"That was amazing. You were just on national TV. Wow. I can say I knew you when."

"We were on TV!" she exclaimed. "*Sparkle* was on TV! This is amazing. I have to call Celeste! Do you know what this means?"

"I hope only good things," he answered.

Warmth trickled through her at the sincere happiness in his voice. He meant his words. He wanted only the best for her, from the very beginning.

How could she possibly go on without this man in her life?

She pushed away the dark thought, focusing instead on this incredible turn of events.

"I have to call the printer and order more books and make more toys and maybe hire more people."

"Take a minute to breathe first," he advised. "You should savor this. You worked hard and you deserve the success. Don't rush past it looking at the tasks ahead of you until you've embraced this moment."

"I've got to record this. How do I do that? I've got to figure out how to do that." She spent a minute trying to work the controls on the DVR and finally got it right just as the door to her bedroom was shoved open and Celeste burst in, eyes wild and her cheeks flushed.

"You need to see the news! We were just on *Hello, Nation*! The *national* news!"

"I know! Rafe called me and I caught it just in time. Did you hear what Paloma Rodriguez said? *Charming and sweet and heartwarming.* That's you she's talking about! Your story. Isn't it wonderful?"

She suddenly realized her sister didn't look convinced of that. She sank down onto the bed, the color beginning to leach out of her cheeks.

"I'm not ready for this!"

She laughed—until she realized Celeste was completely serious. Her sister looked terrified.

"Rafe, I have to go," she said into the phone.

"Okay."

"Thank you for calling. Just...thank you."

"Sure."

He ended the connection and her heart gave a little spasm, wondering when—or even *if*—she would have the chance to talk to him again.

She sat down beside her sister on the bed and gripped Celeste's icy fingers. "This is wonderful news, CeCe. Now everybody else will know how brilliant you are, too. You wrote a beautiful story and it's only right that it has an audience beyond our family, don't you think? What would Mom and Dad say about sharing our gifts, not hiding our light under a barrel? You have an amazing gift and it needs to be out there, glowing for all the world to see."

"That's easy for you to say. You've always been comfortable glowing in the world. To me, this is a terrifying thing."

"It's a wonderful thing," she corrected. "Think of how many people you can touch with your words. Mom and Dad would have been so proud of you, honey."

Celeste gave her a shaky smile, then her eyes filled with tears. "Until you came back, I was perfectly happy writing Sparkle stories for only Barrett and Louisa."

"See? I knew there was a reason I needed to come home."

A reason that had nothing to do with a certain gorgeous former navy SEAL, she reminded herself, and slid from the bed with one more hug for her sister.

"I guess I'd better get dressed. Ready or not, I have a feeling The Christmas Ranch is about to get much, much busier."

Chapter Fourteen

"Are we almost there? I can't believe we're finally here. I finally get to sit on Santa's lap and tell him what I want for Christmas. Do you think I'm too late?"

Rafe glanced in the rearview mirror at Joey, who was just about bouncing out of his seat with excitement. He didn't begrudge the kid a little happiness, especially after the past rough three weeks. As sick as he had been, listless with fever, it was good to see him being excited about *anything*.

The week after Thanksgiving, Joey came down with what Rafe thought was just a virus but it had turned into a nasty bronchitis. Two visits to Dr. Jake Dalton's clinic and a round of antibiotics later, he had ended up missing seven days of school and had only returned for the previous week.

Now, the night before Christmas Eve, this was the first chance they'd had to come to The Christmas Ranch.

Rafe didn't want to endure another few weeks like they'd just passed through. He had a whole new appreciation for the challenges parents faced on a regular basis. Nothing could break a parent's heart like a sick kid.

"The dude in red is pretty good at last-minute orders," he finally answered, "but I can't make any promises. Anyway, we wrote him a letter while you were sick, remember? I'm sure he got that, so you're probably golden."

He was pretty sure he had covered all the Christmas bases, at least from a gift standpoint. The kid's wish list had been short enough, actually, that Rafe had double-checked to make sure Joey had included everything he wanted.

His nephew only asked for a couple of LEGO sets—that Rafe had actually ordered online just after Thanksgiving when they were first mentioned—and a Marvel superhero backpack he had managed to pick up in Idaho Falls the week before, after Joey finally went back to school.

He had found a few other things on that shopping trip—probably too many, actually. He didn't have a good handle yet on appropriate Santa gift quantities. He had even managed to wrap everything over the weekend after Joey went to bed, though none of it would win any prizes in the gift-wrap department.

"I can't wait!" Joey said, then coughed a little with the lingering bronchial spasms he hadn't quite shaken. "What should we do first? The sledding hill or the sleigh rides?"

"Why don't we get the Santa thing out of the way, since that's your first priority, and then you can decide the rest?"

"That's a good idea. Look! There it is!"

Sure enough, the bright and welcoming lights of The Christmas Ranch beat away the dark December gloom. A light snow fell, adding an even more picturesque quality to a scene that already looked warm and festive. He drove beneath the sign he had tacked up for Hope that first day he had come here and was aware of a little bubble of nerves coursing through him.

He was looking forward to this, probably more than he should, given the way things had ended with Hope.

Joey's sickness had been tough enough to cope with this month. Throw in Cami's sentencing the day before and he was definitely in need of a little holiday spirit.

He hadn't seen Hope in more than three weeks, since the Ranch opened. True to his word, he had stayed away as she had asked him. It was just about the hardest thing he had ever done and he was honest enough to admit that he might have caved and gone to see her anyway, if not for Joey's illness.

How many times had he wanted to drive up here, just to talk this out and tell her she was being crazy? He had even turned up the canyon twice after Joey went back to school the week before but had ended up driving past and turning around, feeling like a stupid kid riding his bike past the house of his elementary school crush in hopes of catching a glimpse of her.

He had to drive through the parking lot twice before he found a parking space. The place was hopping, as he had fully expected. That little bit on the national news had spawned all kinds of other publicity. The weekly newspaper in town had done a big spread on The Christmas Ranch and on the runaway success of *Sparkle and The Magic Snowball*, which was racing up bestseller lists after she had digitized it and put it online as an ebook.

He had read every word of the article and had held the newspaper in front of him for far too long, gazing at the photograph of Hope. It was lovely and sweet, a picture in the snow and sunshine with Sparkle all decked out in his holiday jingle bell gear. Even so, he was aware the image had captured none of her vitality and spirit, the energy and enthusiasm and creativity that made her so amazing.

He parked the SUV and helped Joey out of the backseat. His nephew slipped his hand in Rafe's as they walked toward the lodge, which sent a little shaft of warmth settling in his chest.

The illness had at least served one good purpose—he and Joey finally seemed to have bonded over coughing fits and sniffles and nebulizer treatments. His nephew at last seemed to have accepted that Rafe wasn't going anywhere. The night before, he had even told Rafe he thought he was pretty cool. High praise, indeed, from a seven-year-old. It made him feel almost as good as surviving BUD/S.

When they walked inside, they were met with noise and laughter and a jazzy Christmas trio playing in the corner. The scent of pine and cinnamon filled the air.

They made their way through the crowd inside toward the ticket counter, though it wasn't easy. The place was packed as this was the last night the St. Nicholas Lodge was open—though he had read in that article he had all but memorized in the local newspaper that the Nichols family apparently kept the Christmas village open on Christmas Eve with free admission, their gift to the community.

The sleigh rides and sledding hill would continue to operate until after New Year's Eve.

He bought all-access tickets for him and Joey, which would allow them to enjoy all The Christmas Ranch activities. Just as he was hooking the green-and-red-striped wristband on his nephew, Barrett Dustin rushed up to them.

"You're here! Finally!"

"I told you I might be coming tonight," Joey said to the boy who had become his best friend.

"Have you seen Santa yet?"

"Not yet. We just got here."

"I've already sat on his lap like a hundred times but I'll stand in line with you again if you want. Tonight you get M&M's bags instead of just candy canes after you talk to him! I already had one but I want another one."

"Can I, Uncle Rafe?"

"Sure. Go ahead. I'll catch up."

The boys raced off, giggling together. Rafe was fastening his own wrist brace when he became aware of some subtle shift in the atmosphere in the room. Joey—who adored all things Star Wars and had made him watch far too many Clone Wars cartoon episodes while he was sick—would have called it a disturbance in the Force.

He shifted and there she was, just a few feet away from him, speaking with a couple he had met in Jake Dalton's waiting room. Cisco and Easton Del Norte, he remembered, along with their little girl who looked to be about five, chubby-cheeked and adorable, and a very cute toddler little boy.

She must have felt that disturbance in the Force, too—or maybe just the weight of his gaze. Her attention shifted from the couple and for just a split second when she first saw him, he saw a world of emotions in her beautiful blue eyes—shock, discomposure and a wild, unexpected joy.

She blinked away everything and said something to the couple then approached him a moment later. "Rafe. Hello."

He wanted to stand there staring at her all night, absorb every detail he had missed so much. These past three weeks, without her smile and her laughter and that sweet, lovely face, nothing had felt right.

"Hi."

After an awkward moment, she reached out and hugged him in the way of friends who haven't seen each other in too long. He closed his eyes for just a moment, soaking in the scent of her, cinnamon and almonds, and the *rightness* of having her in his arms, even for this quick, meaningless hug.

Too soon, she stepped away, her expression guarded.

"How have you been? How's Joey? I've been worried sick about him."

"He's doing better. Thanks. He's so relieved to finally have a chance to see Santa that I think he would have walked here if I hadn't finally agreed to bring him tonight."

He wanted to make perfectly clear that was the reason he was there, not because he couldn't go another hour without seeing her—though that was probably closer to the truth.

"Oh, and I need to give you a belated thank-you for the care package you sent over with Faith and Barrett when they stopped by. It helped."

She had sent drawing paper and colored pencils as well as a copy of her and Celeste's book and one of her little handmade stuffed Sparkle toys, which he had been afraid his Transformers/IronMan/Anakin Skywalker loving nephew might think too girlish. On the contrary, Joey had been delighted with it, especially because Hope had made it. His nephew had come a long way since calling her mean that day he broke her window.

She smiled softly. "You're welcome."

Before he could respond, a tired-looking woman holding hands with a child on either side of her jostled Hope, who stumbled and would have fallen if he hadn't reached out to catch her.

"Sorry. I'm sorry," the woman said, with a frazzled look. He wanted to tell her not to apologize. In fact, he would have paid her twenty bucks to do it over and over if it would give him the chance to hold Hope in his arms again.

She remained there for a fraction of a moment, gazing up at him with a startled look in her eyes before she swallowed and eased away again.

"Wow," he said. "This place is packed."

She smiled, looking heartbreakingly beautiful. "If I could ever meet Paloma Rodriguez in person, I would smooch her all over her face. Seriously. We've been hopping ever since she featured us on *Hello, Nation*. I've had to hire a dozen temporary workers to keep up with the crowds and I've got eight women in the local quilting guild sewing Sparkle toys for us— and we *still* can't keep up with the orders."

"That's terrific."

He was so happy for her success, mostly because he knew how important it was to her.

"What's going on with Cami?" she asked. "I've been wondering. Was she sentenced this week?"

He nodded grimly. "Yesterday. She got three to five, which was a little longer than her attorney expected, and she won't be eligible for parole for twenty-four months. She was transferred from the county jail to the state penitentiary right after her sentencing, though she got to see Joey for a few minutes before they took her."

"Oh, Rafe. I'm sorry."

He shrugged. "She made a long string of poor choices and they had consequences—one of which is, I guess, that I get to be a father figure for at least the next two years."

"Not a father *figure*. A father."

"Right."

The magnitude of the task somehow seemed less overwhelming than it had a month ago. He figured they would get through it as they had this month— one moment at a time.

"Looks like Joey and Barrett are almost to the

front of the line," she said. "You'd better go if you want to get any pictures for his scrapbook."

"I don't expect I'll have time for much scrapbooking the next few years, but you're right. I should at least take a picture or two to capture the moment."

"Find me before you leave tonight," she said. "I have something for you. I was actually going to bring it over to your house tomorrow but if it's okay; I'll give it to you tonight instead."

That shocked him enough that he wasn't quick enough to come up with a response before she slipped away through the crowd. He watched her for a moment, then turned to freeze Joey's moment with Santa for posterity.

It was too noisy inside the lodge for him to hear what the boy requested from Santa. As soon as his nephew hopped down, he asked him, just to make sure he wasn't missing a big-ticket item on the wish list.

Joey gave him a solemn look. "That's between me and Santa."

He suddenly had fears of the boy coming up with something entirely new, something Rafe wouldn't be able to deliver since he had no idea what it might be. The way he figured it, this was probably the last year the kid would believe in Santa. He was already beginning to express a few qualms about the physical logistics of one man making it all around the world in one night.

Rafe wanted to hold on to the magic as long as he could. He would hate to disappoint the kid in their first Christmas together, especially given all Joey had been through the past few months and the fact that it would be tough enough this first year without his mom.

"Want to give me a hint?" he asked, a little desperately, as they stood in line for the horse-drawn sleigh rides that made up the next thing on Joey's list.

He thought Joey wasn't going to answer him, but as they walked toward Sparkle and the others in their enclosure, he looked up at the sky, speckled with a few stars that peeked out from the clouds, then back at Rafe. "I asked if we could stay here," he finally said. "I like it in Idaho. I don't want to go to San Diego."

He didn't know what to say. "Why not? San Diego is great. It has beautiful beaches and nice weather all year round and lots of fun things to do."

"But it doesn't snow there," Joey said. "I like snow. I like throwing snowballs, I like sledding, I like making snow angels and going on sleigh rides. All those things. I like snow and I like all my friends here. I don't want to leave Barrett or Sam or any of my other friends."

Rafe wanted to tell him he would make new friends, but he had a feeling the promise would sound hollow.

He didn't have a chance to continue the conversation until they were loaded onto the sleigh with several others and the driver started out on a well-worn trail through the snow.

"What did Santa say, when you asked him if you could stay here?"

"He said he couldn't make promises about where people live. It's up to their parents." Joey looked disgusted, his shoulder bumping Rafe's arm as the horses jostled them. "I told him I didn't live with my parents right now and he said it was up to whoever I lived with. He also said sometimes what you think you want is different from what you really need."

The words seemed to hit Rafe with the force of rocket-propelled grenade.

Sometimes what you think you want is different from what you really need.

In his case, he knew what he wanted *and* what he needed—and they were exactly the same thing.

Hope.

He loved her. *That* was the edgy feeling that had been under his skin all this time.

He was in love with Hope Nichols, the scared thirteen-year-old girl he had helped rescue from a terrorist camp in Colombia, another lifetime ago.

This wasn't simply attraction or friendship or affection. He needed her in his life—and Joey did too, he suddenly realized.

He gazed up at the wintry night, at the dark silhouette of the mountains and the full moon that peeked just over the top of them. He loved this place, too, and didn't want to leave it.

Like Joey, he wanted to stay in Pine Gulch.

How could they make it work? He could help her run The Christmas Ranch but it was obviously a seasonal enterprise. What could he do the rest of the year?

He gazed at the mountains, thinking of a hundred possibilities. He was heading back to San Diego to work private security for his friend Jim. Why not see if Jim wanted to open a satellite operation here in

Jackson Hole? He could definitely see a need, with all the wealthy visitors and celebrities who visited there.

If that didn't pan out, he could always start a construction company. The home-building industry in this part of the West was vibrant, spurred by all those celebrities and wealthy folks who wanted to build second homes.

He had no doubt he would come up with something. He had spent seventeen years as a navy SEAL, trained to find solutions to tough situations.

The main job ahead of him would be convincing Hope she needed him too.

Hope couldn't seem to shake her melancholy mood.

She told herself it was only because this was the last night the lodge would be open for the season. After the frenzy of the past month, it was only natural to focus a little on endings, on goodbyes.

Her melancholy certainly had nothing to do with a gorgeous hazel-eyed SEAL or his adorable nephew.

She would miss this, as crazy as things had been since Paloma Rodriguez had changed their world. When the season was over, she would suffer a little bit of a loss. Reviving The Christmas Ranch had given her purpose and meaning and she wasn't quite sure what would happen next.

Right now, she decided to focus on that and not the much larger heartache awaiting her in the form of that particular man she didn't want to think about.

"One of the elves told me you were the one in charge."

She turned at the statement and found a woman in her early thirties. She was quite pregnant but wore a fashionable maternity coat and a lovely knit scarf and matching hat. Behind her stood a handsome, well-dressed man holding a girl of about four while a boy around Barrett and Joey's age stood nearby.

"Yes. I'm Hope Nichols," she said warily, afraid the woman wanted to lodge some sort of complaint. "May I help you?"

The woman's serious features suddenly dissolved into a watery smile. "This is probably going to sound strange but...can I give you a hug?"

"I... Sure."

The woman offered her a quick embrace then stepped away, looking embarrassed. "You must think I'm crazy."

"Not at all," Hope assured her. "Is everything okay?"

At the woman's sudden sniffle, the man handed her a tissue and rubbed her shoulder in a warm, familiar, loving gesture that sent an ache lodging under Hope's breastbone.

She wanted that—the steady comfort of knowing she had someone to lean on when times were hard and someone to celebrate with when wonderful things happened.

"I just have to tell you how grateful I am to you and your family for giving us this treasure. I'm so happy you opened this year after all. It feels like a gift you gave just to me. I was devastated when I heard it was going to be closed early in the season. I... My name is Jane Ross. This is my husband Perry. We live in Pocatello and each year since I was a teenager, my family has come here during the holidays. It was the highlight of our Christmas season."

Hope smiled, heartened to hear what wasn't an unfamiliar tale. *This* was the reason she wanted to open the Ranch, because of families like this that found joy and togetherness here.

"This has been the hardest holiday season for me ever," the woman said softy. "My parents both died within the past year, my mother just a few months ago."

"Oh. I'm so very sorry."

"The holidays have been incredibly tough. I miss them so much and I didn't know how I could bear it. I haven't felt like having Christmas at all. It just seemed like too much work, you know? But I had to anyway." She gave a helpless shrug. "The children needed Christmas. I put the tree up and decorated the house, but I've only been going through the motions, just trying to make it through and crying just about every night because I missed my parents so much. Then I saw an article about you in the newspaper, about how you were going to close because of a recent family tragedy but had decided to stay open after all. I told Perry we had to come and I'm so very glad we did."

The woman squeezed her fingers. "Coming back here," she went on, "bringing my own children and continuing the tradition, I feel such a connection to my parents again. For the first time, I'm remembering the joy and magic and meaning of Christmas again. I can't express how much that means to me. Thank you so much for helping me find that again."

"You are so welcome." Hope embraced the woman again, sniffling a little along with her.

"We picked up one of your books and the Sparkle toy, as you can see."

She pointed to the little girl, who was hugging it tightly.

"You can be sure it's going to be enjoyed for many seasons to come. Merry Christmas and God bless you for what you've given us."

She waved them on, her heart overflowing—and her tears, too.

"That was lovely."

She whirled around and found Rafe standing nearby, looking big and warm and comforting.

"You heard?"

"Most of it. Does that sort of thing happen a lot?"

"Once in a while. That was...special."

She wanted to sink into his arms. It was an almost visceral need. How had she forgotten how happy her heart was when he was near?

"Where's Joey?" she asked, mostly to distract herself.

"Barrett took him up to the house so they could exchange Christmas presents."

"Ah." The crowd was starting to thin, she saw, but it was still packed inside the lodge. "Have you eaten? Aunt Mary brought down a bunch of goodies for all the workers, including a big batch of minestrone soup in the slow cooker. It's kind of our goodbye celebration at the lodge, even though we'll partially reopen up again the day after Christmas."

"I'm not really hungry," he said, a strangely solemn look on his handsome features.

She had missed him desperately. Seeing him again only made her realize just how much.

Her emotions, already raw from the interaction with Jane Ross, threatened to consume her.

She swallowed them down and forced a smile. "I told you I have something for you and Joey. It's back in the office."

He nodded and followed her as she led the way. Inside the office, he closed the door behind him, as if he didn't want to be disturbed, and her heart started to pound.

"I'm...glad you stopped by tonight," she said.

"Even though you asked me to stay away?"

She sighed. She ought to simply hand over the present, wish him Merry Christmas and safe travels back to San Diego and say goodbye.

She wasn't particularly good at doing what she ought to. Why break her record now?

"That was kind of a stupid thing for me to ask of you, wasn't it?"

"If by *stupid*, you mean insanely difficult, then yes."

Something about the intensity of his voice sent her resident troupe of butterflies pirouetting through her insides again.

"It didn't work very well anyway," she muttered and felt his attention sharpen on her.

"What didn't work?"

"Nothing. Never mind. Let me just grab your gift."

She hurried to the corner where she had left the large flat package. "Here you go."

"Thanks."

"Go ahead. Open it."

"Are you sure?"

She wanted to see his reaction. What was the fun

in giving a gift if she couldn't see how it was received? He ripped the paper away and held out the large framed photograph.

"Wow. That's wonderful."

It was of Joey. The boy had his arm around Sparkle's neck and his smile was as big as the brilliant blue sky behind him.

"I shot it one day when you were helping out, before we opened. Isn't it great? I sent it away to be printed on canvas and then I had Mac Palmer, one of our Santas who does some woodworking, make a frame for it out of the extra barn wood we had around the Star N. I wanted both of you to have a keepsake from The Christmas Ranch so you can remember your time here."

He gazed down at the smiling boy and the sweet-faced reindeer, a soft light in his eyes. "It's lovely. Thank you."

"You're welcome."

He didn't return her smile. "One question, though. Do you really think I'm going to need a photograph to remember my time here?"

Her heart started to pound again. "Won't you?"

He set the photograph down on the desk and moved closer to her, those stunning hazel eyes intense, determined. She thought of that nocturnal predator again and a nervous thrill shot through her.

"I could never forget you, Hope."

She swallowed, unable to look away. "Um, sure. We have a...history together."

"I wish we didn't," he said fervently. "I wish I had met you for the very first time that day Joey broke your window."

That would certainly have made their tangled relationship much easier but she couldn't agree. Their lives were inextricably entwined and had been for a long time.

She thought about fate—about how the past and the present could sometimes twist and curl together like ribbons on a Christmas tree.

He had been an integral part of her life since she was a girl—she just hadn't known it.

"Don't say that," she murmured. "Our lives are bound together because of the past."

He reached for her hand and she was stunned to feel his fingers tremble a little, her amazing, hard, tough navy SEAL. "I would rather our lives were bound together because of right now, this moment. Because of our feelings for each other."

She hitched in a breath and met his gaze. "Rafe—"

"I love you, Hope. I knew at Thanksgiving, I just didn't want to face it until you said you were afraid you were falling for me. These past weeks without you only showed me how very cold and empty my life is when you're not part of it. I need you. Your laughter, your energy, your amazing creativity. All of it. I love every part of you."

He gave her a lopsided half smile that completely shattered the last of her defenses. "That's why I wish we'd never met. So we could leave behind all the baggage—the mistakes, the regrets—and simply be two people finding each other at last, like some kind of Christmas miracle."

She couldn't seem to order the tangled chaos of her thoughts into anything resembling coherency. All she wanted to do was kiss him desperately.

At her continued silence, he gave her a long, steady look.

"I know what you said the last time we were together. Hell, I've gone over that conversation in my head so many times I've got every word memorized. Has anything changed? Is there any chance you might be able to accept the past for what it was and see me for who I am right now, today? A man so in love with you, he can't seem to think about anything else?"

She exhaled on a sob that was half laughter, half tears. "Rafe. Oh, Rafe."

She threw her arms around his neck and he groaned a little then kissed her with all the pent-up, aching need she had been pushing back throughout this endless December.

He kissed her for a long time while Christmas music played and the crowd buzzed behind the closed door. She never wanted it to end.

Eventually they came up for air, but she couldn't seem to get close enough to him. She rested her head on his chest—that broad, let-me-take-all-your-troubles chest—and had never felt so safe and warm and loved.

"This has been the craziest month," she murmured. "I can't even tell you. We have been so incredibly busy, every day I hardly had time to take a shower, but the Ranch has had its biggest year ever. Our profits are quadruple what they've ever been. We're going to have enough to more than cover our operating expenses and even to help offset the operating cost deficit on the Star N side of things, too."

"I knew you would do it. Didn't I tell you?"

She smiled, humbled and overwhelmed at his constant faith in her. "Here's the thing. I was so happy that all our hard work paid off and especially happy for CeCe as I watched people fall in love with her writing and want more. I should have been over the moon. But I missed you so much, I couldn't truly enjoy the success. A hundred times a day, I wanted to share some little triumph with you. To laugh with you or be frustrated or get some of that sometimes annoying but usually spot-on advice you always seem to have."

"I'm going to remember you said that."

His laughter was a low rumble against her cheek and she had no choice but to kiss him again.

"I love you, Rafe," she said, some time later. "I loved you and I missed you and Joey so much I could hardly breathe around the ache in my heart. I'm sorry I couldn't be there while he was sick."

"We got through it. Your care package helped. You can be there next time."

She felt a little thrill at the idea—not that Joey would ever get sick again, she didn't want that. But that Rafe wanted her in his life to help him through, if it were to happen again.

"I realized something while we were apart," she said softly. "Since I graduated from college, I have been traveling around the world in search of something I couldn't even name. Oh, I genuinely wanted to make a difference in the world and enjoyed experiencing other cultures, seeing new things, helping people as much as I could in my small way. But something was always missing."

She smiled at him, feeling as if she would burst

from the joy that bubbled through her. "I finally know what it was."

"Oh? Let me guess. Cinnamon hot cocoa."

"Well, that and something else." She smiled tenderly and kissed his jaw. "I'm talking about you, Rafael Santiago. Isn't it funny that I could travel all over the world seeking something without knowing it and I only found it when I finally came back home?"

He pulled her close again and kissed her sweetly, gently, while outside she heard Christmas carols and the sound of children's laughter and the occasional hearty *Ho Ho Ho*. She had done this—brought joy to other people and a little holiday spirit. It had been hard, backbreaking, intense work but worth every moment.

In return, she had received the very best gift of all, the only one that really mattered.

Love.

* * * * *

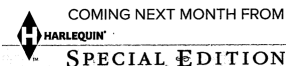

COMING NEXT MONTH FROM

HARLEQUIN

SPECIAL EDITION

Available December 16, 2014

#2377 NEVER TRUST A COWBOY • by Kathleen Eagle

Who's the cowboy on her doorstep? Lila Flynn wonders. The ranch hand who shows up looking for a job is a mystery—and a charmer! Handsome Delano Fox is a man of many talents *and* secrets, and he soon makes himself indispensable on Lila's South Dakota ranch. But can he heal the beauty's wounded heart—without betraying her trust?

#2378 A ROYAL FORTUNE

The Fortunes of Texas: Cowboy Country • by Judy Duarte

Proper British noble Jensen Fortune Chesterfield isn't looking for a lady of the manor...until he gets lassoed by the love of a lifetime! While visiting family in tiny Horseback Hollow, Texas, Jensen falls head-over-Oxfords for quirky cowgirl Amber Jones. They are two complete opposites, but their mutual attraction is undeniable. But can Jensen and Amber ever come together—for better *and* for worse?

#2379 THE HOMECOMING QUEEN GETS HER MAN

The Barlow Brothers • by Shirley Jump

When former beauty queen Meri Prescott returns home to Stone Gap, North Carolina, to care for her grandfather, she's not the same girl she was when she left. Her physical and emotional scars mark her as different—like her ex, former soldier Jack Barlow. He suffers from PTSD after his best friend's death. Can Meri and Jack heal each other's wounds to create a future together?

#2380 CLAIMING HIS BROTHER'S BABY • by Helen Lacey

Horse rancher Tanner McCord returned home to Crystal Point, Australia, to settle his brother's estate...not to fall in love with the woman who'd borne his brother's son. Beautiful Cassie Duncan is focused on her baby, Oliver, but can't resist her boy's loner uncle. As Tanner steps in to care for his newfound family, he might just find his very own happily-ever-after!

#2381 ROMANCING THE RANCHER

The Pirelli Brothers • by Stacy Connelly

Jarrett Deeks knows about healing a horse's broken spirit, but little does the rugged rancher realize that an injured nurse, Theresa Pirelli, will end up mending his broken heart! Theresa is used to curing patients, not being one. But Jarrett's tender bedside manner makes her think twice about returning to her busy life once she is recovered...and staying with him forever.

#2382 FINDING HIS LONE STAR LOVE • by Amy Woods

Manager at a Texas observatory, Lucy keeps her head out of the stars. She's focused on her niece, Shiloh, for whom she is a guardian. Her world is thrown out of orbit when handsome Sam Haynes shows up in town. Sam just found out Shiloh is his long-lost daughter, but he's kept it secret. As he falls for lovely Lucy and sweet Shiloh, can the chef cook up a delicious future for them all?

YOU CAN FIND MORE INFORMATION ON UPCOMING HARLEQUIN° TITLES, FREE EXCERPTS AND MORE AT WWW.HARLEQUIN.COM.

HSECNM1214

REQUEST YOUR FREE BOOKS!

2 FREE NOVELS PLUS 2 FREE GIFTS!

HARLEQUIN®

SPECIAL EDITION

Life, Love & Family

YES! Please send me 2 FREE Harlequin® Special Edition novels and my 2 FREE gifts (gifts are worth about $10). After receiving them, if I don't wish to receive any more books, I can return the shipping statement marked "cancel." If I don't cancel, I will receive 6 brand-new novels every month and be billed just $4.74 per book in the U.S. or $5.24 per book in Canada. That's a savings of at least 14% off the cover price! It's quite a bargain! Shipping and handling is just 50¢ per book in the U.S. and 75¢ per book in Canada.* I understand that accepting the 2 free books and gifts places me under no obligation to buy anything. I can always return a shipment and cancel at any time. Even if I never buy another book, the two free books and gifts are mine to keep forever.

235/335 HDN F45Y

Name _____ (PLEASE PRINT) _____

Address _____ Apt. #

City _____ State/Prov. _____ Zip/Postal Code

Signature (if under 18, a parent or guardian must sign)

Mail to the Harlequin® Reader Service:
IN U.S.A.: P.O. Box 1867, Buffalo, NY 14240-1867
IN CANADA: P.O. Box 609, Fort Erie, Ontario L2A 5X3

Want to try two free books from another line?
Call 1-800-873-8635 or visit www.ReaderService.com.

* Terms and prices subject to change without notice. Prices do not include applicable taxes. Sales tax applicable in N.Y. Canadian residents will be charged applicable taxes. Offer not valid in Quebec. This offer is limited to one order per household. Not valid for current subscribers to Harlequin Special Edition books. All orders subject to credit approval. Credit or debit balances in a customer's account(s) may be offset by any other outstanding balance owed by or to the customer. Please allow 4 to 6 weeks for delivery. Offer available while quantities last.

Your Privacy—The Harlequin® Reader Service is committed to protecting your privacy. Our Privacy Policy is available online at www.ReaderService.com or upon request from the Harlequin Reader Service.

We make a portion of our mailing list available to reputable third parties that offer products we believe may interest you. If you prefer that we not exchange your name with third parties, or if you wish to clarify or modify your communication preferences, please visit us at www.ReaderService.com/consumerschoice or write to us at Harlequin Reader Service Preference Service, P.O. Box 9062, Buffalo, NY 14269. Include your complete name and address.

HSE13R

SPECIAL EXCERPT FROM

HARLEQUIN

SPECIAL EDITION

Jensen Fortune Chesterfield is only in Horseback Hollow, Texas, to see his new niece...not get lassoed by a cowgirl! Amber Rogers isn't the kind of woman Jensen ever imagined falling for. But, as Amber's warm heart and outgoing ways melt his heart, the handsome aristocrat begins to wonder if he might find true love on the range after all...

***

"What...was...that...kiss?" She stopped, her words coming out in raspy little gasps.

"...all about?" he finished for her.

She merely nodded.

"I don't know. It just seemed like an easier thing to do than to talk about it."

Maybe so, but being with Jensen was still pretty clandestine, what with meeting in the shadows, under the cloak of darkness.

The British Royal and the Cowgirl. They might be attracted to each other—and she might be good enough for him to entertain the idea of a few kisses in private or even a brief, heated affair. And maybe she ought to consider the same thing for herself, too.

But it would never last. Especially if the press—or the town gossips—got wind of it.

So she shook it all off—the secretive nature of it all, as well as the sparks and the chemistry, and opened the passenger door. "Good night, Jensen."

"What about dinner?" he asked. "I still owe you, remember?"

Yep, she remembered. Trouble was, she was afraid if she got in any deeper with him, there'd be a lot she'd have a hard time forgetting.

"We'll talk about it later," she said.

"Tomorrow?"

"Sure. Why not?"

"I may have to take my brother and sister to the airport, although I'm not sure when. I'll have to find out. Maybe we can set something up after I get home."

"Maybe so." She wasn't going to count on it, though. Especially when she had the feeling he wouldn't want to be seen out in public with her—where the newshounds or local gossips might spot them.

But as she headed for her car, she wondered if, when he set his mind on something, he might be as persistent as those pesky reporters he tried to avoid.

Well, Amber Rogers was no pushover. And if Jensen Fortune Chesterfield thought he'd met someone different from his usual fare, he didn't know the half of it. Because he'd more than met his match.

***

We hope you enjoyed this sneak peek at
A ROYAL FORTUNE by USA TODAY *bestselling*
author Judy Duarte, the first book in the brand-new
Harlequin® Special Edition continuity
THE FORTUNES OF TEXAS:
COWBOY COUNTRY!

On sale in January 2015, wherever
Harlequin Special Edition books and ebooks are sold.

Copyright © 2015 by Judy Duarte

HSEEXP1214

HARLEQUIN®

A *Romance* FOR EVERY MOOD™

Love the Harlequin book you just read?

Your opinion matters.

Review this book on your favorite book site, review site, blog or your own social media properties and share your opinion with other readers!

Be sure to connect with us at:
Harlequin.com/Newsletters
Facebook.com/HarlequinBooks
Twitter.com/HarlequinBooks

HREVIEWS

HARLEQUIN®

A *Romance* FOR EVERY MOOD™

JUST CAN'T GET ENOUGH?

Join our social communities
and talk to us online.

You will have access to the latest
news on upcoming titles and special
promotions, but most importantly,
you can talk to other fans about your
favorite Harlequin reads.

Harlequin.com/Community

Facebook.com/HarlequinBooks

Twitter.com/HarlequinBooks

Pinterest.com/HarlequinBooks

HSOCIAL

HARLEQUIN®

A *Romance* FOR EVERY MOOD™

Stay up-to-date on all your romance-reading news with the *Harlequin Shopping Guide*, featuring bestselling authors, exciting new miniseries, books to watch and more!

The newest issue will be delivered right to you with our compliments! There are 4 each year.

Signing up is easy.

EMAIL

ShoppingGuide@Harlequin.ca

WRITE TO US

HARLEQUIN BOOKS
Attention: Customer Service Department
P.O. Box 9057, Buffalo, NY 14269-9057

OR PHONE

1-800-873-8635 in the United States
1-888-343-9777 in Canada

Please allow 4-6 weeks for delivery of the first issue by mail.

HSGSIGNUP

JUST CAN'T GET ENOUGH
ROMANCE
Looking for more?

Harlequin has everything from contemporary, passionate and heartwarming to suspenseful and inspirational stories.

Whatever your mood, we have a romance just for you!

Connect with us to find your next great read, special offers and more.

Facebook.com/HarlequinBooks
Twitter.com/HarlequinBooks
HarlequinBlog.com
Harlequin.com/Newsletters

HARLEQUIN®

A *Romance* FOR EVERY MOOD™

www.Harlequin.com

SERIESHALOAD